**Levi wondered if Sarah realized how pretty she was with the new morning light streaming through the window bathing her face in golden light.**

To his eyes, she grew more beautiful with each passing year. It was no wonder Daniel had fallen in love with her.

Levi dropped his gaze to his feet, afraid his thoughts would somehow show in his eyes. "Do you mind?"

"Do I mind what?" she asked at last with an odd inflection in her tone.

He waved his arm to indicate the shop. "That I made changes?"

"*Nee*, it is your work space," she said quickly.

"*Goot.*"

"What needs doing in here today that Grace would normally do? I'm at your beck and call, so put me to work."

"I don't need anything." What he wanted was for her to go home. The workshop was his sanctuary. How could it be a place of peace with Sarah in it?

**Books by Patricia Davids**

Love Inspired

*Brides of Amish Country

Love Inspired Suspense

## PATRICIA DAVIDS

After thirty-five years as a nurse, Pat has hung up her stethoscope to become a full-time writer. She enjoys spending her new free time visiting her grandchildren, doing some long-overdue yard work and traveling to research her story locations. She resides in Wichita, Kansas. Pat always enjoys hearing from her readers. You can visit her on the web at www.patriciadavids.com.

# A Hope Springs Christmas

## Patricia Davids

*Love* Inspired

Recycling programs
for this product may
not exist in your area.

 ™ LOVE INSPIRED BOOKS

ISBN-13: 978-0-373-87781-2

A HOPE SPRINGS CHRISTMAS

Copyright © 2012 by Patricia MacDonald

www.LoveInspiredBooks.com

Printed in U.S.A.

Let your light so shine before men,
that they may see your good works,
and glorify your Father which is in heaven.
—*Matthew* 5:16

This book is lovingly dedicated to my daughter Kathy and her husband, Tony. Thank you for your help and love. You both mean the world to me.

# Chapter One

∽

"You can tell me the truth, dear. How are you really?"

Sarah Wyse dropped her gaze to the pile of mending in front of her on the scrubbed pine kitchen table without answering her aunt. How was she? Frightened.

"Tell me," her aunt persisted. Emma Lapp didn't believe in beating around the bush. She had a sharp eye and a gift for two things, matchmaking and uncovering gossip. How had she found out so quickly?

Sarah had expected to have a few days before having this conversation, but that wasn't to be. "I'm fine, *Aenti* Emma. Why do you ask?"

"You put on such a brave face, child. I know how hard the holiday season is for you. To lose your job on top of everything, my heart goes out to you. You must remember the Lord never gives us more than we can bear. Put your trust in Him."

"All is as God wills, even when we cannot comprehend His ways."

Christmas brought Sarah more painful memories than joy. Too many of her holidays had been marked by funerals. She dreaded the arrival of winter each year with its long, dark, lonely nights. It was her job that kept her sane. *Had* kept her sane.

What would she do now? What if the crippling depression she struggled to overcome got the upper hand?

"How will you manage?" Emma asked.

Sarah raised her chin and answered with a conviction she didn't feel. "As best I can. Would you like some tea?"

"That would be lovely."

Her aunt's sudden arrival was a blessing in disguise. Sarah had been sitting alone in her kitchen, wallowing in self-pity. It solved nothing. She needed to be busy.

She rose and crossed to the cupboard. Taking down a pair of white mugs, she carried them to the stove and filled them with hot water from the kettle steaming on the back of the cooktop.

"I know how you depend on the income from your job, Sarah, being a widow and all. Your *onkel* and I will help if you need it."

"Don't fret for me. It's only for a few months. Janet is moving her mother to Florida and wants to make sure she is settled before coming back. She plans to reopen Pins and Needles after Easter." Surely, she could hang on that long.

Emma cocked an eyebrow. "Will she be back? I heard she might stay."

A flash of panic hit Sarah, but she suppressed it. Janet would be back. Then things would return to normal.

"I'm sure she'll be back. Her business is successful. She enjoys the shop and loves the town. I have ample savings and the income from the rent of the buggy shop. I'll be fine."

Things would be tight, but Sarah would manage financially. Emotionally, that was another story.

Emma said, "Pins and Needles is successful because of

the long hours you put into it. Anyway, you can depend on your family and the church to provide for you."

"I know." Being the object of sympathy and charity again was something Sarah preferred to avoid. She knew her attitude was prideful. Perhaps that was why God had set this challenge before her—to teach her humility.

Emma folded her arms over her ample chest. "You must find something to keep you busy."

"I was making a to-do list when you arrived." Sarah indicated a spiral notebook on the table.

"*Goot.* Have you thought of inviting your brother and his family for a visit? You haven't seen them in several years. The girls will be grown women before you know it."

After having been raised with only sisters, her brother, Vernon, had been blessed with two girls of his own and finally a boy. He and his wife were expecting another child in the spring. It would be good to see them. Having children in the house might help dispel the gloom that hung over her holidays.

"That's a fine idea. I'll write to Vernon first thing in the morning and invite them for a visit. There isn't much room here for the children to play. I hope they won't mind a stay in town." The family lived on a large dairy farm outside of Middlefield where the children had acres of woods and fields to roam.

Emma grinned. "You'll have to take Merle fishing if you want to keep that little boy happy. The last time we went to visit them, that was all he wanted to do and all he talked about. The girls entertain each other."

Sarah suffered a stab of grief. Her husband had liked to fish. It wasn't something she cared for. She should have tried harder to enjoy the things he liked, but how was she to know their time together would be so short?

Regrets were useless, but sometimes it seemed as if they were all she had.

She said, "I'll offer to take Merle on a fishing trip, weather permitting, if that will persuade his parents to come."

Emma chuckled. "He will nag them until they do."

Sarah placed a tea bag in each mug and carried them to the table along with the sugar bowl. As she sat down, a commotion in the street outside caught her attention.

A horse neighed loudly followed by raised voices. "I never want to see you again, Henry Zook! Do you hear me? Go ahead and marry Esta Barkman. See if I care. She—she can't even cook!"

A slamming door from the house beside Sarah's punctuated the end of the outburst.

"Goodness, was that Grace Beachy shouting in the street? Has she no *demut?*"

Oh, dear, her neighbor and friend Grace would soon find her quarrel public knowledge unless Sarah could stanch it. What on earth had Henry done to upset her so? Sarah cast a rueful smile at her aunt. "Grace has humility, *Aenti*. She is normally a quiet, reserved young woman."

"You couldn't tell it from her behavior just now. I understand the twins, Moses and Atlee, are the ones most often in trouble." Emma held her head cocked to hear any additional outbursts.

"They have been a trial to live beside," Sarah admitted as a frequent recipient of the teenage pair's numerous pranks.

The boys had turned seventeen in October. They were in their *rumspringa,* the "running around" years enjoyed by Amish youth from age sixteen up to their mid-twenties prior to taking the vows of the faith. Like many, the twins were making the most of their freedom, but they had always been on the wild side.

Sarah had grown up with an identical twin sister who rivaled the boys for getting into mischief. She missed her sister dearly. Bethany had left the faith to follow her English husband to the other side of the world. They died together in a car accident in New Zealand. In a way, Grace had become a substitute for Sarah's lost sister. She loved the girl.

Emma's eyes were alight with curiosity. "It sounded as if Grace is sorely put out with Henry. It would be a shame if the courtship ended this way. The bishop's son would be a fine match for the Beachy girl. I know Henry's mother is pleased as punch that her wayward son appears to be settling down."

If Grace married and left home, Sarah shuddered to think what the twins would be up to without her intervention. Levi, the eldest of the family, chose to ignore their less than perfect behaviors.

Emma couldn't resist the urge to learn more. "I want to see how Henry is handling this. I can't imagine he's happy to have his girlfriend shouting at him. His mother will want to hear of this."

Rising, she went to the kitchen window that overlooked the street and used her sleeve to rub an area free of frost. Winter had a firm grip on the town of Hope Springs, Ohio, although it was only the first week of December. Peering through the frosty glass didn't give Emma a clear enough view so she moved to open the door.

Sarah quickly stepped between her aunt and the chilly night. Emma's nosy nature knew few bounds. "Leave the young people to sort out their own problems, *Aenti*."

Emma relented but she was clearly miffed at being denied more food for gossip. "How can I tell Esther Zook what happened if I can't see how her son is taking this rejection?"

"I'm sure if Henry Zook wants to discuss it with his mother, he'll find a way."

"She should know how his girlfriend is treating him."

Sarah pressed a hand to her chest and widened her eyes in disbelief. "You don't mean you'll mention this to the bishop's wife."

"I might, if the opportunity presents itself."

"You are a brave soul. I could never bring myself to tell Esther Zook that I heard her son was playing fast and loose with Grace *and* Esta Barkman."

Her aunt nibbled at the corner of her lip, then said, "It did sound that way, didn't it?"

"Grace is a sweet girl and would never raise her voice without serious provocation. I know Esther dotes on Henry and won't hear a bad word against him. I can only imagine how upset Esther would be with someone who spread word of his poor behavior. You know how much sway she holds over the bishop."

Her aunt's frown deepened. "I see your point. We don't actually know what happened, do we?"

"*Nee,* we don't. A lover's spate is all I heard. Not worth mentioning."

"You could be right."

"I know I am." Sarah waited until her aunt gave up trying to see over her and returned to the window. Sarah grinned as she started to close the door. Across the street, she caught sight of Levi Beachy standing motionless at the door to his shop. He'd obviously heard his sister's commotion, too.

His breath rose as white puffs in the cold night air. Their eyes met across the snow-covered street. Sarah couldn't see the color of them from this distance, but she knew they were as blue as a cloudless summer's day. They contrasted sharply with his dark hair and deeply tanned skin.

She rarely saw his eyes, for Levi kept them trained on his feet unless he was working. He was painfully shy, and she wished there was something she could do to help him overcome it. He had been a wonderful help to her when her husband was sick.

A quick frown formed on Levi's face before he turned away with a shake of his head.

"Great, now I'm the one who looks like the nosy neighbor," Sarah muttered. She sometimes had the feeling that Levi disapproved of her, although it wasn't anything she could put her finger on.

"What was that?" Emma asked.

Sarah pasted a smile on her face as she closed the door and returned to the kitchen table to resume her mending. "I saw Levi across the street. He's working late again."

"The poor fellow. He was saddled with raising his younger sister and those unruly brothers at much too early an age. He should have had the good sense to send them to his father's sister or even let his grandfather raise them. Reuben Beachy would have been glad to take care of the children."

Since Reuben was well past seventy, Sarah wasn't sure he would have been able to handle the twins any better than Levi did. "I'm sure Levi loves his family and wants to take care of them himself."

"I don't know how anyone could tell. The man hasn't spoken more than a dozen words to me in all his life. I think he is a bit simple."

Sarah leveled a hard gaze at her aunt. "Levi is shy, not simple."

Emma lifted the tea bag from her mug and added two spoonfuls of sugar. Stirring briskly, she said, *"Even a fool, when he holdeth his peace, is counted wise: and he that shutteth his lips is esteemed a man of understanding. Proverbs 17:28."*

Coming to her neighbor's defense, Sarah said, "Levi works very hard. He builds fine buggies, and he always pays the rent for the shop on time. He is a good man. I don't like to see him maligned."

"Gracious, child. I'm not maligning the man. I know several women who think he would make a good match, but I've had to tell them all that he is a waste of time. Levi Beachy will never find the courage to court a woman, much less propose. I've rarely met a fellow destined to remain an old boy, but Levi is one."

An old boy was the Amish term for a confirmed bachelor. Since only Amish men who married grew beards, a clean-shaven face marked a man as single no matter what his age. Like her, Levi was nearing thirty. She knew because they had attended school together until the eighth grade. She'd known Levi her entire life. He'd been the first boy to kiss her.

That long-forgotten memory brought a blush to her cheeks. Why had it surfaced after all these years? She bent over her mending.

"What about you, dear? It's been nearly five years since Jonas's passing. Are you ready to think about marriage again? I can't tell you the number of men who have asked me that question. One in particular." Emma eyed her intently.

Sarah should have known this wasn't the simple social visit her aunt claimed. She met her aunt's gaze as sadness welled up inside her. For once, she couldn't stop it. Tears stung her eyes. "No, *Aenti*. I've made my feelings on the subject clear. I won't marry again."

\* \* \*

Sarah was laughing at him. She and her aunt were having a chuckle at the expense of his odd family. Levi knew it the way he knew the fire was hot—because he'd been burned by both.

It was wrong to dwell on the past, childish even, but the embarrassing incident came to mind when he least expected it. He'd long ago forgiven Sarah, but he hadn't been able to forget her part in his humiliation.

He had been fourteen at the time and the least athletic boy at school. His shyness made it easy for others to make fun of him, but Sarah had seemed kinder than his other classmates. She sat one row up and across the aisle from him.

How many hours had he spent dreaming about what it would be like to simply hold her hand? Too many.

Then one day, he found a note on his desk saying to meet her down by the creek after school if he wanted a kiss. He'd been ecstatic and frightened all at the same time. Of course he wanted to kiss her. What boy didn't? It took all the courage he could muster to make the short trek to the meeting spot.

She was waiting on the creek bank with her eyes closed just as the note said, but when he caught her by the shoulders and kissed her, she pushed him away. He never knew if it was by design or by accident that the fallen tree limb was right behind him. He tumbled backwards, tripped and landed in the water with a muddy splash.

On the other side of the creek, a dozen of his schoolmates began laughing and hooting, including Sarah's twin sister, Bethany. Mortified, Levi had trudged home in wet clothes and refused to go back to school. Working beside his father in his carpenter shop was the only thing that felt normal to Levi.

Less than a year later, both his parents were killed in a buggy accident. Levi was forced to sell his father's business. No one believed a fifteen-year-old boy could run it alone. Jonas Wyse bought the property and started a harness shop and buggy-making business in Hope Springs. He hired Levi, who desperately wanted to earn enough to support his sister and little brothers. The two men quickly became friends. Within five years, they had a thriving business going making fine buggies. They stopped repairing harnesses and focused on what they did best. It was a wonderful time in Levi's life.

Then Jonas decided to marry Sarah and everything changed.

Levi shook off his thoughts of the past. Sarah was his landlady and the widow of his only true friend. Levi was determined to treat her with the respect she deserved, but he sometimes wished he hadn't promised Jonas he would look after her when his friend was gone. That promise, made on Jonas's deathbed, was a binding one Levi could not break. Not if he planned to face Jonas in heaven one day.

Levi's gaze traveled to the colorful calendar on the shop wall. It was out of date by several years, but he'd never taken it down. His Amish religion didn't allow artwork or pictures to decorate walls, but a calendar had function and even one with a pretty picture was permitted. The one he never removed featured a panoramic view of the Rocky Mountains.

The dusty eight-by-ten photograph showed snow-capped mountains thrusting upward to reach a clear blue sky. Their flanks lay covered with thick forests of pine, aspen trees and spruce. It had long been Levi's dream to move to Colorado. Several of his cousins from the next village had moved to a new settlement out west and wrote in glowing terms of the beauty there. The idea of raising a family of his own in such a place was a dream he nurtured deep in his heart.

Colorado was his goal, but Sarah Wyse was the rope keeping him firmly tethered to Hope Springs.

He had loved Jonas Wyse like a brother. When his friend pleaded with him to watch over Sarah until she remarried, Levi had given his promise without hesitation. A year or so wasn't much to wait. The mountains weren't going anywhere.

It wasn't until Sara remained unmarried for two years that Levi began to doubt the wisdom of making his rash promise. Five years later he was still turning out buggies in Hope Springs and handing over rent money to help support her while his dreams of moving west gathered dust like the calendar on the wall.

He knew several good men who had tried to court Sarah, but she had turned each and every one of them aside. Levi had to admit none of them held a candle to his dear friend. But still, a woman Sarah's age should be married with children.

The thought of her with another man's babe in her arms brought an uncomfortable ache in his chest. He thrust aside thoughts of Sarah and replaced them with worry about his sister.

He hoped Grace was all right. He should go see, but he didn't know what to say to her. Women didn't think like men. Whatever he said would be sure to make her angry or make her cry. Perhaps it would be best to stay in the shop and wait until she called him for supper.

Half an hour later, he heard Sarah's aunt's buggy drive away. He went to the window and looked out. Sarah was alone again, as she was every night. She sat at her kitchen table working on some stitching. Why hadn't she remarried? What was she waiting for?

She was a devout Amish woman. She wasn't too old. She was certainly pretty enough. She kept a good house and worked hard. When the buggy shop needed repairs or upgrades he couldn't do himself, she was never stingy about hiring help or buying new equipment.

As he was looking out the window, he saw his sister approaching. He picked up a file to finish smoothing the edge of a metal step he was repairing.

Grace opened the door. "*Bruder,* your supper is ready."

"*Danki,* I'll be in shortly." He glanced up. His sister didn't leave. Instead, she walked along the workbench, looking over the parts he was assembling for a new buggy. She clearly had something on her mind. When she didn't speak, he asked, "Is everything okay?"

Her chin came up. "Why wouldn't it be?"

*Because you were screaming at your boyfriend at the top of your lungs on a public street and giving our neighbors food for gossip.* "Just wondering, that's all."

"Levi, can I ask you a question?"

He didn't like the sound of that. "Sure."

"Why haven't you married?"

That took him aback. "Me?"

"*Ja.* Why haven't you?"

Heat rushed to his face. He cleared his throat. "Reckon I haven't met the woman God has in mind for me."

"God wants each of us to find the person who makes us happy, doesn't He?" Grace fell silent.

Levi glanced up from his work to find her staring out the window at Sarah's house. Because her question so closely mirrored his thoughts about Sarah, he gathered his courage and asked, "Why do you think Sarah Wyse hasn't remarried?"

"Because she loved one man with her whole heart and her whole soul and she knows no one can replace him," Grace declared with a passion that astounded him.

She suddenly rushed toward the door. "I'll be back in a few minutes. Your supper is on the table."

"Where are you going?"

"I need to talk to Sarah about something."

When the door banged shut behind her, he sighed. It was just like his sister to leave him in the dark about what was going on. He hoped Sarah could help because the last thing he wanted was a home in turmoil, and unless Grace was happy, that was exactly what was going to happen.

After her aunt had gone, Sarah stared at the snow piled on the sill of her kitchen window. Dismal. There was no other word for it. Christmas would be here in less than a month, but there wasn't any joy in the knowledge. The Christmas seasons of the past had brought her only heartache and the long winter nights left her too much time to remember. At least this year her only loss was her job. So far.

She closed her eyes and folded her hands. "Please, Lord, keep everyone I love safe and well this year."

Second thoughts about inviting her brother for a visit crowded into her mind. He was all she had left of her immediate family. At times, it seemed that everyone she loved suffered and died before their time. What if something should befall Vernon or his wife or children while they were here? How would she forgive herself?

No, such thinking only showed her lack of faith. *It is not in my hands, but in Your hands, Lord.*

Still, she couldn't shake a feeling of foreboding.

She opened her eyes and propped her chin on her hand as she stared at the notebook page in front of her. The kerosene lamp overhead cast a warm glow on the mending pile and the sheet of paper where she had compiled a list of things to do.

*Clean the house.*

*Mend everything torn or frayed.*

*Make two new kapps.*

*Stitch the border on my new quilt.*

She had already finished the first item and was on to the second. They were all things she could do in a week or less and she had a lot more time on her hands than a mere week. Spring seemed a long way off. Inviting Vernon and his family was one way to help fill the days.

She added three more items to her list.

*Don't be bored.*

*Don't be sad.*

*Don't go insane.*

Six days a week for nearly five years she had gone in early to open the fabric store and closed up after seven in the evening. Without her job to keep her busy, what was she going to do? Work had been her salvation after her husband's passing.

Had it really been five years? Sometimes it seemed as if he'd only gone out of town and he would be back any minute. Of course, he wouldn't be.

She had tried to convince Janet to let her run the shop until spring, but Janet wouldn't hear of it. Instead, her boss said, "Enjoy the time off, Sarah. You work too hard. Have a carefree Christmas season for a change."

Janet didn't understand. Time off wouldn't make the holidays brighter. Six years ago Sarah and Jonas learned he had cancer only a week before Christmas. He battled the disease for months longer than the doctors thought he could. He died on Christmas Eve the following year. A month later, her sister ran away, leaving Sarah, her parents and her brother to grieve and worry. Their father died of pneumonia the following Thanksgiving. Her mother passed away barely a year later. Vernon said they died of a broken heart after Bethany left.

Bethany had been the light of the family. Her daring sense of humor and love of life were too big for Hope Springs and the simple life of the Amish. It had been two years ago at Christmas when Jonathan Dresher came to tell Sarah that Bethany was dead, too. Since that day, Sarah faced the Christmas season with intense dread, waiting and wondering what the next blow would be.

She sat up straight. She wasn't going to spend this winter cooped up in the house, staring at the walls and dreading Christmas. She had to find something to keep the bleak depression at bay. To her list, she quickly added *Find Another Job!* She circled it a half dozen times.

The sound of her front door opening made her look up. Like most Amish people, she never locked her doors. Knocking was an English habit the Amish ignored for they knew they were always welcome in another Amish home. A brief gust of winter wind came in with her visitor. Sarah's mood rose when she recognized her friend and neighbor, Grace Ann Beachy.

*"Gut-n-owed,"* Sarah called out a cheerfully good evening in Pennsylvania Deitsch, sometimes called Pennsylvania Dutch, the German dialect spoken by the Amish.

"Sarah, I must speak to you."

Sarah was stunned to see tears in Grace's eyes. Fearing something serious had happened, Sarah shot to her feet. "Are you okay?"

*"Nee,* I'm not. I love him so much." Grace promptly buried her face in her hands and began sobbing.

Sarah gathered the weeping girl in her arms. Matters

of the heart were often painful, but never more so than when it was first love.

"There, there, child. It will be all right." Sarah led Grace to the living room and sat beside her on the sofa. The two women had been friends for years. They were as close as sisters.

Between sobs, Grace managed to recount her evening with Henry Zook from the time they left the singing party. The whole thing boiled down to the fact that Henry had grown tired of waiting for Grace to accept his offer of marriage. The conversation soon turned to a quarrel. Henry, in a fit of anger, said Esta Barkman had been making eyes at him all evening. Maybe she was ready to settle down and marry.

Sarah lifted her young neighbor's face and wiped the tears from her cheeks. "If you love him, why don't you accept him? Is there someone else?"

Grace rolled her eyes and threw up her hands. "There's Levi and the twins and the business. How can I leave my brothers? Levi can't manage the business alone. He can barely speak to people he knows. He's terrible at taking care of new customers. They'll go elsewhere with their business and where will that leave him? You depend on the income from the shop, too."

"Your brother could hire someone to replace you. I know Mary Shetler would welcome the chance to have a job in an Amish business."

"I'm not sure she would want to work with the twins, knowing what they did."

Grace was probably right about that. Mary Shetler had left the Amish and wound up living with an English fellow who turned out to be a scoundrel. Just fifteen and pregnant at the time, Mary had been terrified to learn her boyfriend planned to sell her baby. She had the child alone

one night while he was gone. Planning to leave her boyfriend for good as soon as she was able, she hid her infant daughter in an Amish buggy along with a note promising that she would return for her.

The buggy belonged to Levi Beachy. The twins had taken it without permission and sneaked out to see a movie in another town. It wasn't until they were on their way home that they discovered the baby. Afraid their midnight romp would get them in trouble if they brought the infant home, they stopped at the nearest farmhouse and left the child on the doorstep in the middle of the night.

Fortunately, the home belonged to Ada Kauffman. Her daughter Miriam was a nurse. She and Sheriff Nick Bradley finally reunited mother and child but not before Mary suffered dreadfully believing her daughter Hannah was lost to her.

"All right, Mary was not a good suggestion, but I'm sure there are other young women who could work with Levi."

"Maybe, but what about the twins? They could burn the town down or who knows what if someone doesn't keep an eye on them. I know I haven't done a great job, but I'm better than Levi. When he's working, he could be standing in five feet of snow and not notice. I can't leave knowing no one will look after them."

"I'm sorry you feel trapped by your family, Grace. You know I would help if I could."

Grace grabbed her arm. "You can."

"How?"

"Help me find a wife for Levi."

# Chapter Two

Sarah stared at Grace in stunned disbelief. "You must be joking. How could I find a wife for your brother? I'm no matchmaker."

"But you are," Grace insisted. "Didn't you convince your cousin Adrian Lapp to court Faith Martin?"

"Convince him? *Nee,* I did not. If I remember right, I cautioned Faith against losing her heart to Adrian because he was still grieving for his first wife." Sarah knew how it felt to mourn for a spouse.

"And that was exactly the push Faith needed to see beyond his gruff behavior. They married, and they are very happy together. Besides, you're the one who convinced me to give Henry a chance."

"I don't remember saying anything to you about going out with Henry."

"If you hadn't told me how your Jonas settled down from his wild ways after you were married, I never would have given Henry the time of day. But I did, and now I'm in love with him. I want to marry him. You have to help me. I will just die if he marries someone else."

Sarah leveled a stern look at her young neighbor. "That's a bit dramatic, Grace."

Drawing a deep breath, Grace nodded. "I'm sorry. I don't know what to do. I can't leave Levi and the boys, but I can't expect Henry to wait forever, either. I'm caught between a rock and a hard place with no way out."

"I hardly think finding a wife for your brother is the answer."

"It's the only one I can come up with. I'm afraid if I ask Henry to wait much longer he'll find someone else."

Sarah took pity on her young friend and tried to reassure her. "Henry Zook will not marry anyone else. I've seen the way he looks at you."

"I believe he loves me. He says he does, but he wants an answer."

"Henry is used to getting his own way. His mother has done her best to spoil him. He will be a good man, but right now he has the impatience of youth. What you and Henry need is a cooling-off time."

"What do you mean by that?"

The last thing Sarah wanted was to see her friend pushed into something she might regret. "You two have been seeing each other almost daily. I think both of you could use some time apart. Rushing into marriage can cause a lifetime of misery."

Grace shook her head. "Oh, Sarah. I don't know. What would Henry think?"

Sarah could see that Grace's dilemma was taking its toll on her friend. There were shadows beneath her eyes that didn't belong on a girl who was barely twenty. Her cheeks were pale and thinner, as if she'd lost weight. There had to be some way to help her. Suddenly, an idea occurred to Sarah.

"He can't object if you tell him you're going to visit your grandmother in Pennsylvania. I know you've wanted to see her for ages. It will give Henry a chance to miss you while you're gone, and it will give you a chance to relax and think about what you want to do without worrying about Henry or about your brothers."

"But what if Henry doesn't miss me?"

"Wouldn't you rather know that before you are wed?" Sarah asked gently.

"*Grossmammi* has asked me to come for a visit many times. She's getting on in years. I would like to spend some time with her, but that means I would miss the quilting bee for Ina Stultz and the hoedown that's coming up."

"I'll take your place at Ina's quilting bee, and there will be other hoedowns. Of course, once you marry, that kind of fun is over." To marry, an Amish couple had to be baptized into the faith, which meant their running-around time was ended. Barn parties and such gatherings would give way to family visits and community events that bound together all members of their Amish faith.

"What about the business?" Grace asked.

"Levi will understand that you need some time to make up your mind about marrying. Besides, he's a grown man. He can manage without you for a few weeks. I can help if worse comes to worst. I used to work there every day."

"Oh, it'll come to worse very quickly. I don't doubt you could do all that I do, but what about your job?"

"The fabric shop is closing for a few months, so I have some extra time on my hands." A lot of extra time, but was working beside Levi the way she wanted to spend it?

Grace's face lit up. She grabbed Sarah's hand. "You are so clever. You can work with Levi and find out what kind of wife would suit him all at the same time. I won't feel a bit bad about leaving him, knowing you're there."

Sarah held back a smile. If this is what it took to get Grace to leave town for a few weeks, Sarah would agree. "I hadn't thought of it that way, but you may be right. In spite of the fact that Levi was Jonas's friend and has been my neighbor for years, I don't really know him well."

Grace sat back with a satisfied smile. "I can tell you anything you want to know about him. Go ahead, ask me something."

"All right, what does Levi like to do for fun?"

A furrow appeared between Grace's eyebrows. "He doesn't really do anything for fun. He doesn't have a sense of humor, that's for sure. He works in the shop all day and sometimes late into the night."

"I know he is hard-working, but does he like to hunt or play checkers or other board games?"

"I don't think so. I mean, I've known him to go hunting in the fall when we need meat, but I don't think he enjoys it. The boys and I like board games, but Levi doesn't play with us."

*What kind of wife would want a husband who didn't interact with his own family?* Sarah said, "He used to go fishing with my husband. Does he still do that with his friends?"

"He goes fishing by himself sometimes. Levi doesn't really have friends. Everyone says he makes right fine buggies, though."

Sarah knew that for a fact. She drove one he and Jonas had built together. It was solid and still rode well after eight years. However, Levi had to have other traits that would make him attractive to a potential wife. "What does your brother like to read?"

"He reads the Bible every night, and he reads *The Budget.*"

*The Budget* was a weekly newspaper put out by the Amish for the Amish. Everyone read it. It was good to know he read the Bible. A devout man usually made an excellent husband. "Does he read other kinds of books?"

"Books? No, I don't think so." Grace shook her head.

Sarah never suspected Levi was such a dull fellow. What had her outgoing husband seen in him?

"You've been a big help, Grace. I'll look over my list of single friends and think on who might find him appealing." Right off hand, she couldn't think of anyone.

"Do you really believe I should leave town?"

"I do. It will do you, your grandmother and Henry a world of good. Trust me on this."

Grace nodded bravely. "I do trust you, Sarah. I'll do it."

Sarah grinned. "That's the spirit."

Grace jumped to her feet. "I must ask the Wilsons down the block if I can use their phone. I need to find out when the bus leaves and call my grandmother's English neighbors so they can tell her I'm coming."

"But it's getting late, child. You should go home and talk this over with your family."

"*Nee.* If I'm to do this it must be now." She leaned down and pressed a kiss on Sarah's cheek. "You're the best friend ever, Sarah Wyse."

Without a backward glance, she rushed out as quickly as she had rushed in, slamming the door behind her.

"I'm not sure your brothers are going to feel the same," Sarah said to the empty room.

Levi tugged his suspenders up over his shoulders as he walked down the stairs from his bedroom on the second floor of the house. When he reached the kitchen, he paused. Instead of the usual aromas of toast, bacon and scrambled eggs, the forlorn faces of his twin brothers sitting at a bare table greeted him.

A suitcase sat beside the front door. His sister, Grace, entered the room, tying her best bonnet beneath her chin. "I left sliced ham in the refrigerator for sandwiches. You boys can heat some up in a skillet for breakfast if you'd like or make oatmeal. After today, you're on your own as far as getting something to eat. There is plenty of canned fruit and vegetables in the cellar along with canned meats. If you don't want to cook, the Shoofly Pie Café serves good food, and it's reasonable."

She picked up her suitcase and gave her younger brothers each a stern look. "I expect the house to still be standing when I return."

Levi found his tongue. "Grace, what are you doing?"

"I'm going to visit *Grossmammi* for a few weeks." She had a smile on her face, but it was forced.

He scowled at her. Grace was impulsive, but this was odd even for her. She hadn't said a word about visiting their relative. "Is Grandmother ill? Is that why you're going?"

"*Nee,* she's fine as far as I know."

"You can't take off at the drop of a hat like this."

Atlee spoke up, "That's what we told her."

"But she told us she was going and that's that," Moses added.

Grace's smile faded. "Please, Levi. Don't forbid me to go. I need you to understand that I have to get away for a while."

How could he understand when she hadn't told him anything? He opened his mouth but nothing came out. She took it as his consent and her smile returned. He never could deny her what she wanted. She and the twins had lost so much already.

She rushed to his side and pressed a kiss to his cheek. "Thank you, Levi. Sarah said you would understand. I've got to run or I'll miss my bus. This was a wonderful idea. I'm so glad she suggested it. I can't wait to see *Grossmammi* again."

Sarah suggested it? He should have known. "Grace,

who will take care of our customers?" he asked as panic began to set in. He couldn't deal with people. Words froze in his mouth and he looked foolish.

"Sarah will help you. Be kind to her." Grace gave him a bright smile as she opened the door. A flurry of cold air swept in as she went out.

When Levi blinked he was still standing in his kitchen not really sure what had just happened. He looked at his brothers. They both shrugged.

Atlee said, "I'd like dippy eggs with my ham."

"I want mine scrambled." Moses folded his hands and waited.

Levi stared at the black stove with a sinking feeling in his gut. How on earth would they manage without Grace?

An hour later, Levi left the house and headed for his retreat, his workshop, where nothing smelled like burnt ham or charred eggs and he couldn't hear his brothers' complaints. He'd left after telling them to do the dishes.

*A body would have thought I told them to take the moon down and polish it the way they gaped at me.*

When he left, they were arguing over who should wash and who should dry. He didn't have time to referee because he was late, and he was never late opening his business.

He still didn't know why Grace had to leave town so suddenly. He hoped she hadn't gotten herself in trouble. That wasn't the kind of thing a man wanted to ask his sister. All Atlee and Moses knew was that after an argument with her boyfriend, Grace had decided to visit their grandmother for a few weeks. How many was a few? Three? Four? She didn't intend to stay away for a month, did she?

One thing Grace said stuck in Levi's mind. She'd said Sarah had suggested it. He suspected that Sarah Wyse was a whole lot better informed about his sister's abrupt departure than he was.

Two men in Amish clothing were standing in front of his store when he approached.

"Did you decide to sleep in today, Levi?" one man joked.

Levi tried to think of a snappy comeback, but nothing occurred to him. He kept his eyes down and wrestled with the key that refused to unlock the door.

"Reckon he wants to start keeping banker's hours," the second man said with a deep chuckle.

Levi hated it when people made fun of him. He searched his heart for forgiveness and offered it up to God, but he still felt small. He always felt small.

When the stubborn lock finally clicked open, he rushed inside. He hadn't had a chance to get the stove going and the building was ice-cold. The two men waited by the counter while he stoked the fire. When he had a flame going, they both stepped up to warm their hands.

Levi cleared his throat and asked, "How can I help you?"

The outside door opened, but Levi couldn't see who had come in. The men blocked his line of sight. He hoped it was the twins because he didn't like dealing with customers. Not that the twins would do better. They were likely to pull some prank and then disappear, leaving him to deal with the fallout.

The taller of the two men said, "We're wanting to order a pair of courting buggies for our oldest boys. They're good sons and they are willing to help pay some of the cost. Before we place any orders, what kind of deal can you give us for ordering two buggies together?"

Levi scowled. "A buggy costs what a buggy costs."

"That's not what Abe Yoder over in Sugarcreek told us. He's willing to take ten percent off for a double order."

Levi struggled to find the right thing to say. Grace

always knew just what to say. Why did she have to take off and leave him to work alone? She knew how much he hated dealing with people.

Abe Yoder's offer was a good one, but Levi didn't want to send these men back to his competition. He couldn't cut ten percent off his price or he'd be making the buggies for free. He cleared his throat again and felt heat rising in his face. Why was it always this way? Other people didn't have trouble talking.

Behind the men, a woman's voice said, "If Abe Yoder says he can cut ten percent off he's overcharging to begin with."

The men turned around as Sarah Wyse approached the stove. She was looked straight at him. "Isn't that right, Levi?"

He nodded and followed her lead. *"Ja."*

She waited, as if expecting he would say more, but when he didn't she gave her attention to the men. "Come up to the counter, neighbors, and let us talk about what you think your sons will like and what they can live without. Once we have an idea of the amount of work that will be needed, we can give you a fair estimate. You'll find our prices are as good as Abe Yoder's and our quality is better."

Levi blew out a breath of relief. Everyone's attention was on her and not on him. Now he could think.

She stepped behind the counter and began opening drawers. "If I can just find our order forms."

"Top left." Levi supplied the direction she needed.

She opened the correct drawer and said, "Ah, here we are. Changes can be made later, but that may affect the price once we've started work. Do you know what color of upholstery they want on the seats? Do they want drum brakes? How about cup holders and storage boxes? I assume these will be open buggies as you said they are for courting."

She waited, pencil posed, with a friendly smile on her face that could charm anyone. Levi was grateful for her intervention until he remembered that she had sent Grace out of town in the first place.

Once again, Sarah seemed bent on making his life difficult.

## Chapter Three

Sarah took down the information the men provided along with their addresses and promised them an estimate would arrive in the mail in a few days. They left, content with that.

When the door closed behind them, Sarah found herself alone. Levi was nowhere in sight. Silence surrounded her except for the occasional crackling and pop of the fire in the potbellied stove. She had time to look around. This cavernous building had been Jonas's favorite place.

There was nothing fancy about the shop. The bare rafters were visible overhead. Thick and sturdy, the wooden trusses were old and stained with age and smoke. A few missing shingles let in the light and a dusting of snow that had melted into small puddles here and there.

Buggy frames in all stages of completion were lined up along one side. Wagon wheels were everywhere, leaning against the walls and hanging from hooks. Some were new and some were waiting to be repaired. Wheel repair made up the bulk of their business. A good buggy wheel could last five years or more, but eventually they all needed to be fixed or replaced.

Down the center of the shop were two rows of various machines. Although their Amish religion forbade the use of electricity, in their church district it was possible to use propane-powered engines to operate machinery. While some of the equipment was new, much of it was older than the hills.

Sarah walked to the ancient metal bender and grasped the handle. The bender used heavy-duty iron gears and wheels to press bands of steel into symmetrical rings. The steel ring was then welded together to form the outside rim of a wagon wheel.

How many rims had she cranked out when she worked beside Jonas and Levi? Two hundred? Three hundred? She could still do it, but it would take a while to build up her muscles. Carrying bolts of fabric wasn't nearly as physical.

Turning around, she noticed the back of the shop held various pieces of wood waiting to be assembled into buggy tops and doors. In the far corner of the building, an area had been partitioned off and enclosed to make a room for cutting and sewing upholstery. The old sewing machine was operated with a foot pedal. She knew it well.

Although almost all the buggies they made were black, as required by their church, a person could order anything from red velvet to black leather for the buggy's interior and seats. Jonas's courting buggy had dark blue velvet upholstery. When he sold it two years after their wedding she cried like a baby.

She smiled at the memory, but she wasn't here to relive the past. She went looking for Levi. Would he have something to say about her usurping his authority in dealing with customers? She found him working on the undercarriage of a buggy at the very back of the building. Or rather, she found his feet.

The sole of his left shoe was worn through. He had used a piece of cardboard inside to keep his socks dry.

Did his socks have holes in them, too? She imagined they did for the hems of his pant legs were worn and frayed. Grace was wrong. Levi didn't need a wife. He *desperately* needed a wife.

Someone with housewifely skills to mend and darn for him and to make sure he was properly clothed. Someone to insist he get new shoes for the winter instead of making do with cardboard insoles. She'd paid no attention to the business books after Jonas died, preferring to leave all that in Levi's hands. Was the business doing poorly? Or was Levi frugal to the extreme?

Clearly, it was time she got her head back into the business. "Levi, may I speak with you?"

A grunt was her answer. Was it a yes grunt or a no grunt? Only his feet moved as he struggled with some hidden problem. She decided to be optimistic. "I'd like to take a look at the ledgers."

His feet stilled. "Why?"

She crouched down trying to see his face. "I realize that I've left the running of the business to you alone for far too long. We are partners in this, are we not?"

He wiggled backward out from under the carriage and sat up to glare at her. "I don't cheat you."

She pressed a hand to her chest. "Goodness, I never thought you did. I simply want to begin doing my share again. Jonas and I used to do the books together. I know what I'm looking at."

"Jonas is gone. I do the books now." He lay down and started to inch back under the buggy.

Sarah was sorely tempted to kick the sole of his miserable excuse for a shoe, but she didn't. More flies were caught with honey than with vinegar. "I don't mean to step on your toes, Levi, but I am the owner of this shop,

and I have a right to see the books. I'm sure you understand my position."

"Help yourself," came his muffled reply.

"Fine." She left him to his work and headed for the
small enclosed place that was used as an office. A wooden
stool sat in front of a cluttered desk. Off to one side, a stack
of ledgers and catalogs were piled together. She started by
searching through them, but soon realized they weren't
what she needed.

She went back to his feet. "Where are the current
ledgers, Levi?"

"Ask Grace."

She blew out a huff of frustration. "I can't very well ask
Grace. She's on her way to Pennsylvania."

He came out from under the frame and rose to his feet.
"*Ja*, she is. I wonder why my sister chose to go running
off during our busiest season with inventory to do and
four carriages to finish. No, wait. I know why she left.
You told her to go."

It was the longest speech he'd ever spoken to her. Sarah
curbed her ire at his tone. "Grace didn't tell you why she
went to visit her grandmother?"

"All she said was that it was your idea."

"Oh." No wonder he seemed upset. Where should she
start?

He folded his arms and stared at his shoes. "Is Grace
in…trouble?" he asked, his voice low and worried.

"Trouble? You mean… Oh! No, no, it's nothing like
that. I hope she would confide in me if that were the case.
No, she and Henry have gotten serious so quickly that I
thought a short cooling-off time would give her a chance
to decide if she really wanted to marry him or not."

"Marry? Grace?"

Levi looked astonished by the idea. It was almost comical. Sarah struggled to hold back a smile. "That's what young people do when they've been courting."

"She's too young to marry." He turned to his tool chest and grabbed a second wrench.

"She's the same age I was when Jonas and I married. I was twenty and he was twenty-seven."

"That was different." Levi didn't look at her.

"How?"

"It just was. Grace Ann is a child." He returned to his position under the buggy.

"*Nee,* Levi, your *shveshtah* is a grown woman. You must be prepared for her to marry and start a family of her own."

A second grunt was her reply.

If Levi hadn't considered where his sister's courtship was leading, then Sarah really had her work cut out for her. Not only did she need to find a woman who could put up with his stoic ways, she needed to help him see that Grace was an adult. This could certainly make the coming winter months more interesting.

Sarah stared at Levi's worn-out footwear. First things first, who did she know that might be ready for a husband?

Several women came to mind. There was the current schoolteacher, Leah Belier, a sweet-tempered woman in her late twenties. But having had the twins in school until two years ago, would she be willing to take them on a permanent basis? It would take a brave woman to do that.

It was too bad Susan Lapp had married Daniel Hershberger last month. While it was an excellent match for both of them, Susan would have been perfect for Levi. Big-boned and strong with a no-nonsense attitude, Susan was a woman who could keep Levi and the twins in line with one hand tied behind her back. Yes, it was too bad she was already taken.

There was Joann Yoder, but she was a year older than

Levi. Sarah couldn't see them together. Joann was nearly as shy as he was.

Mary Beth Zook was also a possibility. Sarah wondered how the bishop and his wife would feel about two of their children marrying into the Beachy family. Perhaps Mary Beth wasn't the best choice, but Sarah didn't rule her out.

Another woman who came to mind was Fannie Nissley, the niece of David and Martha Nissley. She had come to Hope Springs to help the family when Martha had been injured by an overturned wagon a few years before. Martha was fully recovered, but Fannie stayed on because she liked the area.

Sarah guessed her age to be twenty-five or -six. As far as she knew, Fannie wasn't seeing anyone. This coming Sunday after the prayer service would be a good time to find out for sure. Aunt Emma would know if any of the single women in the area had already made a commitment.

Sarah suddenly thought of Sally Yoder. Sally currently worked for Elam Sutter in his basket-weaving business. Sally was only in her early twenties, but she might be ready to settle down. She had a good head on her shoulders and could help Levi manage the business.

Sarah looked around the building and remembered the many hours she and Jonas had spent poring over the company books and inventory, trying to stretch a nickel into a dollar to make ends meet. They hadn't seemed like good times back then, but now she cherished every moment she and her husband had spent working and struggling together.

God took him too soon.

Memories, both good and not so good, filled her mind. As she looked around, it was easy to see traces of Jonas everywhere. The chair where he sat as he ordered supplies was still waiting at the counter, as though he might return at any minute. Of course, Levi used it now.

The workbench Jonas made from scrap lumber had stood the test of time, but it had been shifted from its original position. So had the boxes of parts that once lined the wall above it. Now, they stood along the west wall, closer to where the bulk of the woodwork for the buggies took place. It was a better spot, and she could see why Levi had done it.

She said, "You have made many changes in here. I see you moved the workbench to beneath the south windows. Was that for better light?"

He didn't answer. Sarah crossed to the workbench Jonas had fashioned and laid her hand on the worn wood. She could almost feel him here beside her. Looking out the window, she realized that Levi had an unobstructed view of the narrow street outside and of her kitchen window across the way.

How many times had she sat at that table and cried, worried and prayed since Jonas's passing. Had Levi seen it all?

She glanced toward the buggy frame. He was no longer underneath it. He stood, wrenches in each hand, watching her with a guarded expression on his face.

Levi wondered if she realized how pretty she was with the early morning sunshine streaming through the window, bathing her face in golden light. Her features were as delicate as the frost that etched the corners of the glass behind her.

Her white *kapp* glowed brightly, almost like a halo around her heart-shaped face. Her blond hair, carefully parted in the middle and all but hidden beneath her bonnet gave only a hint of the luxurious beauty her uncut tresses must hold. Only a husband and God should view a woman's crowing glory. For a second, Levi envied Jonas's right to behold Sarah's hair flowing over her shoulders and down her back.

The ribbons of her *kapp* were untied and drew Levi's attention to the curve of her jaw and the slenderness of her neck. To his eyes, she grew more beautiful with each passing year. It was no wonder Jonas had fallen in love with her.

Levi dropped his gaze to his feet, afraid what he was thinking would somehow show in his eyes. She was his best friend's wife. It was wrong of him to think of her as beautiful.

"Do you mind?" he asked.

When she didn't answer, he looked up. She glanced out the window and then at him.

"Do I mind what?" she asked with an odd inflection in her tone.

He waved his arm to indicate the shop. "The changes?"

"*Nee,* it is your workspace," she said quickly.

"*Goot.*" He returned his tools to the wooden tray and carried it to the workbench, sliding it into its place on the end of the counter where Jonas had kept it.

Levi hadn't been much younger than the twins were now when the local sheriff brought word that their parents were dead. They had both drowned when their buggy was overturned and swept away while they had been trying to cross a flooded roadway.

Jonas had come to the house and offered Levi a job when he was ready. Levi never forgot Jonas's kindness in treating him like an adult, like a man with responsibilities instead of like a boy who needed someone to look after him and his siblings.

As Jonas taught Levi the buggy-building trade, Levi had quickly realized Jonas would have been smarter to hire someone who already knew the business rather than an untried teenager.

When he mentioned his thoughts on the subject, Jonas had laid a hand on Levi's shoulder and said, "I want to work with someone I respect and enjoy being around. You and I are a good fit. Besides, if I teach you how to do a thing, I know it will be done right."

Levi never forgot that moment. He became determined to learn everything Jonas had to teach so that his respect was not misplaced. In that, Levi believed he had succeeded.

Sarah had followed Levi to the counter. She asked, "Do you mind my helping out until Grace returns?"

"Not much choice," he conceded gruffly.

"I'm sorry that my advice to Grace sent her racing off so quickly. I honestly thought she would talk it over with you and the two of you could decide when a good time for her visit would be. I didn't mean for this to happen."

"Grace can be impulsive." To his surprise, it wasn't all that difficult to talk to Sarah. His throat didn't close around the words and keep them prisoner as it usually did.

She laughed aloud at his comment. "That's an understatement."

Levi cringed and felt the heat rush to his face. Was she laughing at him or with him? Did it matter?

Sarah said, "I'm at your beck and call, so put me to work. What needs doing in here today that Grace would normally do?"

What he wanted was for her to go home. The workshop was his sanctuary. How could it be a place of peace with Sarah in it? She disrupted everything, including his thinking.

He said, "Nothing I can't handle." Now maybe she would leave.

"I can at least clean up." She turned around, grabbed a red rag from the box he kept them in and began straightening his workbench, moving his tools around and brushing at the bits of loose wood on the countertop.

He didn't like people touching his stuff. "Don't mess with my tools."

She paid him no mind. "I'm not messing with them, I'm cleaning off your workspace."

"Stop," he pleaded.

She held up a lone drill bit. "Where does this go?"

"Take it home with you," he snapped abruptly.

He shut his mouth in horror. He'd never spoken harshly to anyone.

Sarah stared at him for the longest moment and then chuckled with delight. "You are so amusing, Levi. And Grace told me you don't have a sense of humor. Take it home with me, how funny. I'll find where it goes. You get back to work and pretend I'm not even here."

Like that was possible. He turned away before he said something he would surely regret.

She kept dusting. "I'll have this cleaned up in no time. I remember how to do inventory, too. It won't be long before the end of the year. Might as well get a jump on it. I'll start on that when I'm done with this."

"No need." Inventory would take days. Days with Sarah underfoot wasn't something he wanted to endure. He needed to be able to concentrate. She didn't take the hint.

"I don't mind. I'd forgotten how much I enjoy being out here. Don't you love the smell of leather and wood? It's comforting knowing that each piece on the walls around me has a place and a function. I'm glad I told Grace I would help. This place could use some sprucing up, though."

Jonas had often said that Sarah had a one-track mind when she wanted to do something. Levi didn't know how true that statement was until three hours later when she was using a long-handled broom and an overturned bucket to reach cobwebs that had hung from the rafters longer than she had been alive.

Unless he took her by the arm, led her to the door and locked it behind her, he was going to be stuck with Sarah until Grace returned.

*Please, Lord, let Grace's visit be a short one.*

Levi drew a deep breath. It was almost lunchtime, and he hadn't gotten nearly enough done. His eyes were constantly drawn to where Sarah was working.

He had orders to fill and much to do in the coming weeks. When there was snow on the ground, many Amish families brought their farm wagons and buggies in to be repaired while they used their sleighs. With Christmas less than a month away, he was sure to get swamped with work soon.

Moving to the carriage body he was working on, he studied the list of accessories Grace had written out for him to add. The buggy was for Daniel Hershberger's new bride. The well-to-do businessman was sparing no expense for his wife's buggy. As Levi marked out the wood for the extra-sturdy seats to be added, Sarah began humming a hymn. After a few bars, she began singing softly. She had a lovely voice, soothing and sweet.

Levi gripped his handsaw and drew it back and forth across the board. The sound blocked Sarah's voice and he stopped.

She must have noticed because she asked, "Does my singing bother you?"

He looked toward her and found her watching him intently. "*Nee,* it's nice."

She gave him a sweet smile and went back to work,

humming as she did so. Maybe having her around for a few weeks wouldn't be so bad after all.

The outside door opened and Henry Zook walked in. He nodded to Sarah and crossed the room to stand in front of Levi. "I must speak with Grace. Is she about?"

Levi could feel his throat growing tight. This was not a conversation he wanted to have. He cast a speaking glance at Sarah. This was her doing. She would have to make it right.

## Chapter Four

Sarah caught the look Levi darted at her. It was imploring, half-accusing. He clearly wanted her to take over the conversation with Henry. Instead, she retreated to his small office to give the men some privacy.

Yes, it was her fault that Grace had left town so quickly, but Levi needed his eyes opened to exactly how serious Henry was about Grace.

The office had four walls but no ceiling to separate it from the rest of the building. She had no trouble hearing their conversation.

"Please, Levi, I must to speak to Grace. It's important."

"You can't." Levi's reply was barely audible.

"What do you mean, I can't?"

"She's gone."

"Gone? Gone where?" Henry demanded.

"She took off with her handsome English boyfriend early this morning." A new voice entered the conversation.

"*Ja,* he was driving a fine red car."

Sarah was so startled to hear the voices of the twins that she leaned around the doorway to see where they were. She hadn't heard them come in. How long had they been inside?

"Yup, bright red his car was," Atlee agreed with his brother. "Took off with the tires throwing gravel every which way. Grace didn't look none too sad to be leaving this place."

They both sat on the seat of a wagon waiting for repairs with identical smirks on their faces. They elbowed each other with mirth.

Poor Henry. He looked from Levi to the twins with growing disbelief. "Grace would not do such a thing."

The boys hooted with laughter. Moses said, "Proves you don't know our sister as well as you think."

Why didn't Levi say something? Sarah was ready to intervene when Levi spoke at last. "Enough!"

The twins fell silent, but didn't wipe the smiles off their faces. It was clear they didn't think much of their sister's suitor.

"Grace went to visit our grandmother." Levi walked away from Henry as if the conversation was over.

Henry wasn't about to leave without more of an explanation. He followed Levi into the office, forcing Sarah to back into the corner. "Grace never mentioned going out of town for a visit. Has your grandmother taken ill?"

*"Nee,"* Levi replied and pulled open a drawer to search for something. Sarah found herself stuck in the small room with both men for there wasn't enough room to get past them. They both ignored her.

Henry raked a hand through his thick blond hair. "Then I don't understand. Why would she suddenly leave without letting me know? We had a disagreement, but I didn't think she was that upset."

Levi jerked a thumb in Sarah's direction. "Ask her."

Levi found the sheet of paper he was looking for and walked out of the office, leaving Sarah to face Henry alone. He waited for her to speak, confusion written across his face.

Sarah squared her shoulders and indicated the empty chair beside the desk. "Henry, sit down."

He took a seat. "When is Grace coming back?"

"I'm not sure when she'll be back."

"But she will be back, right?" His eyes pleaded for confirmation.

"Of course. She needs some time to think things over without feeling pressured."

He blew out a long breath. "I'm a *nah*. I shouldn't have pushed so hard."

Sarah smiled gently. "You are not a fool, Henry. You're in love. You are impatient to be with her as a husband. That is only natural. Grace has many concerns, but she says that she loves you. If she is the woman God has chosen for you she is worth waiting for."

"I could accept that if I knew how long she wants me to wait. She won't set a date."

He glanced over his shoulder and lowered his voice. "I know she is worried that her family can't manage without her. Can you convince her she has to start thinking about what is best for her?"

"That's exactly what she is doing. If you love her, you must trust her. I suggest you write her and tell her how you feel."

"I feel confused."

Sarah gave him a sympathetic smile. "Do not fret. Things will work out. Now, go home and write Grace a long letter telling her how much you miss her, how sorry you are for your impatience and how you look forward to seeing her again."

"I'm not all that good with words, Frau Wyse."

"They are in your heart, Henry. Look for them there."

He nodded and rose to his feet. "*Danki.* I will do that."

When he left, she walked out into the area where Levi and the twins were putting the top on a buggy. When they had it set in place and bolted on, she said, "I have chicken stew simmering at my house. Levi, if you don't have other plans you are welcome to eat with me for I know Grace usually does all the cooking."

The twins rushed toward her. "We're starving," they said, together.

She held up a hand to stop them. "Psalm 101:7. *He that worketh deceit shall not dwell within my house: he that telleth lies shall not tarry in my sight.*"

The boys looked at each other. "What does that mean?" Moses asked.

Levi walked by with a small grin tugging at the corner of his mouth. "It means you're on your own for lunch. *Danki,* Sarah. I'll be happy to break bread in your home."

"But we were only teasing Henry," Atlee insisted.

"*Ja,* it was a joke," Moses added.

"It was cruel, and you took pleasure in his discomfort. But I forgive you, and I'm sure Henry will, too, when you ask him." She turned to follow Levi out the door.

"So we can eat with you?" Moses called after her.

Sarah paused at the door and looked back at their hopeful faces. She smiled at them. "No."

Their shocked expressions were priceless. She softly closed the door behind her.

Levi opened Sarah's front door and allowed her to go in ahead of him. The mouthwatering smell of stewing chicken and vegetables made his stomach grumble. His poor breakfast had been hours ago.

Sarah said, "You can wash up at the sink. It will only

take a few minutes to get things ready. Are you upset that I refused to feed the twins?"

His family never asked him if their actions were upsetting. He wasn't sure what answer Sarah wanted to hear. He chose, hoping for the best. *"Nee."*

"I'm glad. I don't want you to think that I intended to discipline them without asking your permission. I simply wanted to make it clear to them that actions have consequences. They were intentionally unkind to Henry."

He turned on the water and picked up a bar of soap from the dish. As he washed his hands, the scent of lavender mingled with the delicious smell of the cooking meal. He held the bar close to his nose. It smelled like Sarah, clean, fresh, springlike.

He put the soap down and quickly rinsed his hands. He dried them on a soft white towel hanging from a rod on the end of the counter. It didn't feel right using her things.

When he turned around, Sarah was staring at him. She asked, "You do understand, don't you?"

He hadn't been listening. "What?"

"Why I told the twins they couldn't eat here."

"Sure."

She waited, as if she expected him to say something else. Nothing occurred to him. He slipped his hands in the front pockets of his pants. Could he feel more awkward? Not likely.

Nodding, she said, *"Goot.* Sit."

She indicated the chair at the head of the table. Jonas's place. Okay, that was going to feel more awkward.

Levi pulled his hands from his pockets and took a seat. Sarah moved around the kitchen, gathering plates and silverware. He rubbed his hands on the tops of his thighs. He was hungry, but he hadn't realized how intimate it would feel eating alone with Sarah. They weren't doing anything wrong. He knew that, but being this close to her set his nerve endings buzzing like angry bees.

Even sitting in this chair felt wrong. It was Jonas's chair. It didn't matter that Jonas was gone. It didn't seem right to take the place that was once his. Memories of their last hours together poured into Levi's mind.

He could hear Jonas's hoarse whisper as plainly as if they were back in the upstairs bedroom before his death.

*"Watch over Sarah when I'm gone, Levi. Promise me you'll watch over her until she decides to remarry."*

*"You'll get better."*

*"Nee, my time is up, my friend. God calls me home. I want Sarah to find happiness with someone again, though I pray she doesn't remarry in haste. I know women who have and regretted their decision."*

*"Sarah was wise enough to choose you in the first place. She'll be fine."*

*"You know my Sarah well. I'd rest easier knowing she loved someone strong, from a good family, with a fine farm or business. Promise me you'll watch over her until she meets him, Levi. Promise me this. It's all I ask of you."*

Sarah set a glass of fresh milk on the table, jarring Levi's mind out of the past. He picked up the glass and took a long drink. Her gaze remained focused on his arm.

He stopped drinking. "What?"

"I can mend that rip in your sleeve right quick if you'll slip your shirt off."

He turned his arm trying to see what she was talking about and splashed milk out of his glass in the process. Embarrassed, he looked for something to clean it up with. She was quicker, placing a kitchen towel over the puddle and trying hard not to laugh. Why was he so clumsy when she was around?

"Sorry," he muttered.

"Don't worry about it. Accidents happen. Shall I fix your sleeve?"

He didn't care if his entire arm was hanging out of his clothes. He wasn't about to take his shirt off in front of her. He muttered, "Grace will fix it later."

"All right." Sarah then carried a steaming black kettle to the table and placed it in front of him. She returned a few seconds later with a plate of freshly sliced home-baked bread and a tub of butter, setting them within his reach. She took her seat and bowed her head.

Levi did the same and silently said the prayers he dutifully prayed before every meal. When he was finished, he looked up and waited. Sarah kept her eyes closed, her hands clasped. He cleared his throat. She took it as the sign the prayer was finished. Looking up, she smiled at him and began ladling steaming pieces of chicken and vegetables into his bowl.

She was so pretty when she smiled. It did funny things to his insides.

She said, "I hope you like this. It was one of Jonas's favorites. The recipe belonged to his mother."

Levi suddenly found his appetite had fled. He laid his spoon down

Sarah's eyes filled with concern. "Is something wrong?"

"This is Jonas's place, his chair. I shouldn't be here."

"Levi," Sarah said gently, "I miss him, too, but his place is with God in heaven. You are free to sit in any chair in this home. You were Jonas's friend, and I hope you are my friend, too. He would welcome your company as I do. I know you were very fond of him."

He had been more than fond of Jonas. He had loved Jonas like a brother. When Jonas gave him a job, Levi had no idea what a great friend and mentor Jonas would become. All these things ran through his mind, but he had no idea how to tell Sarah what Jonas meant to him.

She patted his arm. "It's okay. He was fond of you, too. He would like it that you have come to eat at his table. He would be upset that I haven't invited you sooner. Now eat, or your food will get cold."

Levi nodded. He was here for a meal and nothing more. He wasn't here to try and replace Jonas. He could never fill those shoes.

After eating in silence for a few minutes, he said, "You should give Grace this recipe. It's a whole lot better than her chicken stew."

Sarah laughed. Levi felt his face grow red. Had he said something stupid? Once again she touched his arm. It was as if touching came easily to her. It wasn't that way with him. He felt the warmth of her hand even through the sleeve of his shirt. It spread to the center of his chest and pooled there.

She chuckled and said, "I have given this recipe to Grace. She has assured me that everyone in the family enjoyed it. Maybe what she needs is a few cooking lessons."

She wasn't laughing at him. Levi was able to smile, too. "She needs more than a few. Her biscuits are as heavy as stones."

He fell silent again.

Sarah said, "I hope you've saved room for some peach pie. I made it last night."

"Peach is my favorite."

"Mine, too." She smiled warmly at him.

They finished the rest of the meal in companionable silence. When he was done, Sarah rose and began gathering up the dishes. "I'll bring the rest of the stew to your house this evening. I'm sure the twins will be even hungrier by supper time."

He pushed back the chair and stood. "The meal was *ser goot*, but I must get back to work."

"I will be over as soon as I finish these dishes. Is there anything special you need me to do?"

He shook his head, but then changed his mind. "If customers come in, I would appreciate your help finding out what they want so I don't have to stop work each time."

"I can do that. I'll keep watch out the window while I finish up here. If I see anyone I'll come right over."

Levi nodded his thanks and walked out the door.

Sarah watched him go with a strange sense of loss. There hadn't been a man at the head of her table since Jonas's passing. While it felt odd, it also seemed right that Jonas's best friend should have been the one sitting in his place. He'd been like a little brother to her husband. Levi grieved for Jonas as strongly as she did.

Since Jonas's passing, she often felt that Levi was avoiding her. Maybe it wasn't because he disapproved of her. Maybe it was simply that she reminded him too much of his loss.

Sarah shook off the sadness that threatened to bring tears to her eyes and instead concentrated on a plan to see which one of her single friends might be right for Levi, and most important, how to get them together.

It wasn't like Levi was going to attend the singings or gathering that were held on Saturday and Sunday evenings so the young people of the community could mingle and met potential mates. He was past that age and so were the women she had in mind for him.

Levi rarely left his work place, so if Levi wouldn't come out, she needed to find a way to get the women to come in.

The meal today gave her an idea. She would invite her friends, one at a time of course, to join her for a meal when

Levi was present. She would have to include the twins and
Grace, too, when she returned, but that couldn't be helped.
It would look odd if she only asked Levi to come to dinner.
People would say that she was running after him herself.
That wouldn't do.

Perhaps having him and his family over to eat wasn't
such a good idea. Who knew how many times she'd have
to invite them before he found someone he liked? The
twins could put away a lot of food.

Maybe she could ask her friends to help with inventory.
That would be logical excuse to have them spend the day
where Levi was working. She might even convince some
of them to come in and look over the used buggies that
Levi had for sale or buy a new one. If she remembered
right, Leah Belier's buggy was old and worn. Sarah could
drop a few hints about a good price and then leave Levi
to show the teacher what was available. That might work.

Satisfied that she had a few plausible reasons to get Levi
to spend time with some eligible women, Sarah closed the
door and began to clean up the kitchen. While she might
be new at matchmaking, she had been around her aunt
Emma enough to know how it was done. If all went well,
Levi would find a woman to take care of him and Grace
would be free to marry.

Sarah placed the glass Levi had used in the soapy water.
His shirtsleeves were threadbare, and his shoes had holes
in them. He did need someone to look after him.

So why did the idea of Levi getting married suddenly
cause an ache in her heart?

The twins were seated inside Levi's office when he returned to the shop. "Was it a fine meal?" Moses asked.

"Fine enough."

"Better than our church spread sandwiches, I reckon," Atlee grumped.

Levi loved the peanut butter and marshmallow crème spread served for Sunday lunches after the prayer service. "About that good, I guess. Did you finish the wheel we're fixing for Gideon Troyer?"

"Not yet, but we got the fire going good outside," Atlee said in a rush.

"And we finished the upholstery on the front seat for the Hershberger buggy," Moses added. The boys exchanged a lively glance. It was rare that they did work Levi hadn't asked them to do. Perhaps Sarah's scolding had paid off.

"*Danki*. We'd best finish the wheel, though. Gideon will be by to pick it up this afternoon."

"I don't get him." Atlee shook his head.

"Me neither," Moses added.

Levi looked at his little brothers. "What do you mean?"

Atlee said, "He traded in flying airplanes to go back to driving a horse and buggy. Why?"

Levi understood their confusion. Very few of the young men who left the Amish came back and were content to do so after being out in the English world for as long as Gideon had.

From the doorway, a man said, "The outside world held many things that drew me away, but I discovered God's will for me was to return to my Amish roots."

Levi turned to see Gideon walking toward him. He liked the man that had married their cousin Rebecca and not only because he'd helped her regain her sight after years of blindness. He was a likeable fellow in his own right.

Atlee said, "You came back because of a woman."

Gideon gave a sharp bark of laughter. "God's ways are wondrous to behold, as I'm sure you will discover when you are older. Your cousin Rebecca's love was the prize I won for following God's will rather than my own."

Levi looked down at his feet. "Your wheel's not done."

"Mind if I hang around while you finish it?"

"*Nee.* It won't take long." Levi moved toward the side of the building where he assembled the finished wheels. The steel rim Gideon was waiting on had been welded together but it needed to be placed around the wooden rim.

Levi carried the steel ring along with a pair of tongs and a large mallet outside where the twins had build a fire in the pit they used for heating the metal. The flames had died down to a bed of coals that glowed bright red. Levi could barely stand the heat on his face as he laid the steel circle on it. Stepping back, he waited for the fire to do its work and expand the metal.

Moses carried the wooden wheel out and laid it on a scarred slab of wood near the pit. He looked at Gideon. "Tell us what it was like to fly in a plane. Were you scared to be so high?"

Gideon cocked his head to the side as he regarded the boy. "Why would I be scared?"

"Because you might fall out of the sky," Atlee answered.

Gideon grinned. "Falling out of the sky doesn't hurt you."

"It doesn't?" Atlee and Moses looked at each other in disbelief.

"No. Not a bit. It's that sudden stop when you hit the ground that hurts." Gideon winked at Levi as the twins groaned at his joke.

Levi chuckled. "That's a *goot* one."

As the boy begged Gideon for stories about flying, Levi concentrated on watching the fire. He knew the rim was ready when it began to glow red. He motioned to Atlee. He and the boy thrust the tongs into the hot coals from opposite sides and together they lifted the rim from the fire. They carried it to the waiting wheel. Because the heat had expanded the metal, Levi and Atlee were able to slip it over the wooden rim. Levi laid his tongs aside and hammered the steel into place.

Quickly, as the wheel started to catch fire, Moses came with several buckets of water and began dousing it. The hot metal hissed. Steam rose up in a thick fog. After a few minutes, Levi lifted the wheel by the rungs and set it in a water trough. He turned the wheel rapidly to make sure it cooled evenly.

A friend of the twins called to them from the street and they both ran out to talk to him, leaving Levi to finish the work alone. Again.

After a few minutes, he pulled the wheel out of the water and checked the fit over the wooden fellows. It looked good. No gaps, his weld was solid. He was pleased with it. It would last many years. He rolled the wheel to Gideon who inspected it carefully, as well. Levi looked up to see Sarah had come out of the shop.

Gideon spied her at the same moment. "Sarah, how nice to see you."

She gave him a warm smile. Too warm, Levi thought as a frown formed on his face.

"Gideon, you're just happy to see me somewhere besides the shop where your wife spends all your hard-earned cash on fabric for her quilts."

"You have that right. What are you doing here?"

"Helping Levi for a few weeks while Grace is out of town. The fabric shop is closed for the winter, if you didn't know." She moved to stand close beside Levi. He caught a whiff of her lavender soap and drew in a deep breath of it. His heart began racing.

Gideon said, "We heard about the closing. Rebecca was

bemoaning the fact that she will have to go all the way to Sugarcreek for her quilt backing. I reckon she'll wear out a couple more buggy wheels this winter traveling over there. Because, according to her, a woman can never have too much fabric."

"I'm sure my boss would agree with her."

Looking at Levi, Gideon said, "You're a lucky man to have such a pretty helper, for even a few weeks. How much do I owe you?"

Levi said, "Sarah will write up your ticket."

Sarah blushed. Rising on tiptoe, she leaned close and whispered in his ear. "I don't know how much to charge him."

Her warm breath caressed the side of Levi's neck and sent every nerve ending in his body into high alert. He hugged his mallet to his chest and struggled to find his voice. "On the counter."

She leaned closer. "On the counter, what?"

"Paper…with prices."

"*Danki.* I'll go find it, and I'll fix that shirt later." She gave him a bright smile and hurried toward the shop's back door.

He closed his eyes; thankful and sorry all at the same time that she was gone. He reached for his tongs.

Gideon grabbed his wrist. Levi looked at him in surprise and then glanced down at his hand. Comprehension dawned. Levi had been about to grab the end that was still smoking hot. Gideon had saved him from a nasty burn.

He nodded his thanks. *"Danki."*

Gideon glanced from Levi's face to Sarah's retreating form. He chuckled and let go of Levi's wrist. "It's like that, is it?"

Levi frowned. "What do you mean?"

"I was the same way when I realized I was falling for

Rebecca. I fell, literally, at her feet on an icy street. Love makes it hard for a man to concentrate."

"Me? Falling for Sarah? *Nee,* it is not so." Levi shook his head violently.

Gideon laughed. "Whatever you say, my friend. Many men with two good eyes are blind to the desires of their hearts."

# Chapter Five

As Gideon walked away, Levi sought to dismiss the man's disturbing words. Gideon had seen something that didn't exist. Levi refused to think about his feelings for Sarah because he didn't have any past his responsibility to her. Her behavior that day at the creek, not to mention her marriage to his best friend, had put an end to his infatuation.

No, Gideon was wrong. Levi was not in love with Sarah, and she clearly was not love with him. Only a fool would think she would consider Levi Beachy as a replacement for Jonas Wyse, the finest man Levi had ever met.

He carried his tools inside to put them away, determined to think no more about it. The problem he was determined to ignore was seated at the counter with her chin propped on her hands. She smiled sweetly at him, and his foolish heart skipped a beat.

She said, "I found the price list. I don't know why I never noticed it before."

He swallowed hard and nodded, not sure he trusted his voice to answer her.

Sitting up straighter, she said, "Of course, I haven't been in here in the last few years, so perhaps it is understandable. I'll try to learn where everything is so that I don't have to interrupt you with a lot of questions."

"I don't mind." Levi couldn't believe those words actually escaped his lips. He didn't want her questions. He certainly didn't want her to whisper them in his ear.

The memory of her closeness, the way he could smell her freshness, the sensation of her warm breath against his skin was enough to send heat rushing through his body once more. "I must to get to work."

"I understand. I'll stop talking. You can pretend I'm not even here."

He'd already learned that wasn't possible. He would forbid his sister to leave in the future.

"When Grace decides to marry, you'll have to hire a replacement for her. Someone with a sunny disposition would be nice. Can you think of anyone who might interest you? As a replacement for Grace, I mean."

*"Nee."* He didn't want to think about Grace marrying, either. Turning around, he walked to the back corner of the building and started his lathe. The noise of the grinder would cover any more comments by Sarah. He began to work with vigor, building new wheel hubs as fast as he could shape the blocks of wood.

Sarah heaved a sigh of exasperation as Levi busied himself as far away from her as possible. Trying to figure out what kind of wife would suit him would be next to impossible if he wouldn't say more than a dozen words to her.

He hadn't been exactly talkative during their meal, but perhaps in his own home he would open. He and the boys would appreciate her cooking while Grace was gone, she was certain of that.

She could seek information about Levi's likes and dislikes from the twins, but involving them came with its own set of drawbacks. They were bright and inquisitive. They might put two and two together and foil her plans by telling Levi what she was up to. Would he mind?

She didn't know, and she hoped she never had to find out.

She finished the day by getting things ready to do the inventory the following week. Only two customers came in and their requests were easy to handle. Levi managed to stay out of her way completely. No matter where she went, he was just leaving the area with long determined strides. Who would believe they couldn't exchange as much as a sentence when they were both inside the same building all afternoon? It was almost like he was *trying* to avoid her. Was he still angry about her advice to Grace?

Rather than become discouraged, Sarah grew more determined. She would discover the real Levi Beachy if it took her all winter.

Admitting only a temporary setback, she stopped trying to corner the man and settled herself with paperwork in the office. As she went through the previous year's records, she was pleased to see Levi was an excellent bookkeeper. While Grace might take care of the public part of the business, Levi clearly managed the rest with a deft hand. It was something a prospective wife would be impressed with.

When five o'clock rolled around, Sarah went home and gathered what she would need to feed the Beachy family supper. Along with the leftover stew, she packed a loaf of bread and two jars of vegetables she had canned from her own garden. She added a second loaf of bread when she remembered the appetite her brother had during his teenage years.

She carried the makings of the meal to the house next door with a simmering sense of excitement. No wonder her aunt Emma enjoyed matchmaking. Sarah had no idea how exciting it was. Her somber mood and worry about the season had taken a backseat to her enjoyment of the challenge she faced.

Levi had seen her coming. He held open the door. She squeezed past him, brushing against his side in the process. "*Danki,* Levi."

His face flushed deep red. "I—I forgot something."

He rushed out the door, leaving her staring after him. Really? Could he not sit still even in his own home? Miffed that he had once again escaped her, she turned back to see his brothers sitting at the kitchen table, looking at her with wide, hopeful eyes. They resembled a pair of starving kittens in front of an empty milk saucer.

"*Gut-n-owed,* Sarah," they said together.

"Good evening," she replied.

Atlee said, "We're right sorry we upset you with our teasing Henry Zook today."

She inclined her head slightly. "It's forgiven and forgotten. As long as it doesn't happen again."

Moses said, "It won't. When you pull a good joke on a fellow, it's only funny the first time. He might be expecting it a second time."

She leveled a stern gaze at him. "If you have no remorse, I can take supper home with me."

Stifling a grin at their frightened expressions, Sarah glanced at the large box in her arms and the basket hanging on her elbow. "Your supper will appear much faster if I could get a little help."

They were up like a shot and took her burdens from her. They set everything on the counter and stood aside. Sarah began unloading her goods. To her surprise, the countertop was grimy. The stove was, too. She ran a finger along the back edge of the counter.

This much cooking grease hadn't accumulated in a

single day. Grace clearly didn't devote much effort to housework. Poor Henry. He would be in for a shock after the wedding if Grace didn't improve. His mother's home was always as neat as a pin.

Sarah tried to remember the last time she'd been in the Beachy home. It had been years. Grace was forever dropping by to visit at the fabric shop or coming to Sarah's house. After Jonas's death, Sarah had curtailed her visits to friends and neighbors. It became too hard to pretend she was doing better when she wasn't.

She added one more item to her mental to-do list for the winter. Help Grace get her house in order.

The twins had been smart enough to make sure there was a fire going in the stove. Sarah put on the apron she'd brought with her and got to work. It wasn't long before the smell of steaming beets, buttered carrots and chicken stew filled the small kitchen. Glancing over her shoulder, she noticed the boys were hovering near the table but they hadn't taken a seat.

She lifted the lid on the stew and stirred the contents. "It's almost ready. Will you set the table?"

An alarming amount of clatter followed her request. When she turned around, plates, cups and flatware had been haphazardly set for three places.

"You don't want me to eat with you?" she asked sweetly.

The twins looked at each other. Atlee said, "I reckon that will be okay."

"If Levi says it is," Moses added.

She arched an eyebrow. "Perhaps one of you should go ask him."

Moses elbowed Atlee. "You go."

Atlee rubbed his side. "Why me?"

Folding her arms, Sarah asked, "Does Levi object to company?"

Atlee started toward the door. "I don't know. We never have any."

How had this family become so isolated in the midst of a generous and caring community? "Surely, your grandfather and your cousins come to visit on Sundays and at the holidays."

Atlee shook his head. "We normally go to their homes. It's more fun and the food is better. Grace isn't a great cook."

Sarah said, "It's nice to know that Levi enjoys visiting his family."

At the door, Atlee said, "Levi never goes if he can help it. He don't like it when people make fun of him."

"Why on earth would your family make fun of Levi?"

Moses grimaced. "Grace said he used to stutter when he was little. Our cousins and other kids made fun of him back then."

Sarah vaguely recalled Levi's affliction. Was that why he never spoke much? "He doesn't stutter now."

"Now, he doesn't say much of anything. Our uncle calls him Levi Lockjaw," Atlee said and went outside.

Sarah turned back to the stove and resolved to treat Levi with more kindness in the future. She hadn't realized how much of a loner he'd become after Jonas's death. Then again, how could she? She had been wrapped up in her own grief and worries, unable to focus on anything but her work.

The outside door opened a few minutes later. Atlee returned without Levi. "Brother says you may eat here, Sarah. We're to go ahead. He said he'll fix something for himself later."

"He's not coming in?" she asked in amazement.

Atlee shook his head and took a seat at the table.

Sarah pondered the turn of events as she dished up the

meal. Did Levi have that much work to do, or was he simply avoiding her?

The twins fell upon the food like starving dogs. Sarah barely touched hers. Was her company so distasteful that Levi would rather spend the evening in a cold building instead of at his own table if she were there?

If that were the case, she would leave. She stood and carried her plate to the sink.

"Where are you going?" Atlee asked.

"Home. I'll see you both tomorrow at church." She gathered her belongings, grabbed her coat from the hook beside the door and went out.

Instead of going home, she entered the shop by the back door. Only one overhead lamp had been lit. It cast a soft glow where Levi sat on a stool at his workbench. He had a new hub wheel in a vise and was chiseling out the slots for the spokes. He hadn't heard her come in so she had a chance to study him as he concentrated on his work.

What she noticed first about him was his hands. He had sturdy hands, scarred by years of work at his craft, yet he wasn't clumsy. His movements were sure and deft. His body was relaxed, not tense the way he had carried himself all day.

She decided not to interrupt him. Before she could slip back out the door, he suddenly stiffened. She realized he'd caught her reflection in the window glass.

Gathering her courage, she came forward with her icy fingers gripping each other. "I wanted to let you know I was leaving so that you could come in and eat your supper before it grows cold or the twins devour it."

*"Danki."* He didn't turn around but kept his back to her.

She couldn't leave like this. She didn't want him angry with her. "I'm sorry, Levi."

"For what?"

She waved her hands in a helpless gesture. "Everything. I'm sorry Grace took off and left you in a lurch, but mostly I'm sorry that you're angry with me."

"I'm not angry with you," he said quietly.

"You're not?" She took a step closer. When he didn't say anything else, she moved to stand at the counter beside him. She gestured toward the hub he held. "You do good work."

"I'm not angry," he said again.

"It feels like you are. You won't look at me. You wouldn't come in to supper. Something is wrong. Is it because I can't do the work as well as Grace?"

*"Nee."*

She held her frustration in check. "Talk to me, Levi. I don't know what to change if you don't tell me. Do I have to get a blackboard so you can leave me messages?" she teased, trying to get him to smile.

"It's a joke to you, isn't it?" he asked stiffly.

Her teasing had backfired. "Of course not."

"Grace, the twins, me, we're all a joke to you."

"Levi Beachy, what a mean thing to say. Grace is my dear friend. The twins frequently make me cringe or smile, but I don't see them as a joke. I see them as outgoing, boisterous boys."

"I saw you and your aunt laughing at Grace and Henry's argument. I reckon everyone will be talking about my sister's poor behavior tomorrow."

She sighed. So that was it. "Levi, I was grinning at my own cleverness because I had convinced my aunt not to mention the incident."

He cast a sidelong glance of disbelief at her. "You did?"

"Grace is my friend, Levi, just as Jonas was your friend. I had hoped that you and I could be friends, too."

He was silent for so long that she realized she had her

answer. For reasons she didn't understand, Levi wouldn't accept her friendship. The knowledge hurt.

"I'll write to Grace and ask her to return as soon as possible. I'm sorry for the trouble I've caused." She turned to leave.

"Sarah, wait."

She stopped and looked back. His bright blue eyes were gazing intently at her. A strange quiver centered itself in her chest, causing a catch in her breath.

He said, "I am now, and have always been, your friend."

The catch moved to her throat. "I'm sorry I didn't recognize that. Thank you, Levi."

"It's what Jonas wanted."

He was right. Jonas would have wanted them to be friends. Why didn't that cheer her? Perhaps because she wanted Levi to like her for herself and not because of her husband.

Early the next morning, Sarah decided to walk to the church service instead of driving her buggy. The preaching was being held at the home of David Nissley and his wife, Martha. Their farm was little more than a quarter of a mile beyond the Hope Springs town limits.

A warm southern wind was melting the snow, making the sunshine feel even brighter. Rivulets of water flowed in the ditches, adding occasional gurgling to the symphony of morning sounds that surrounded her. Numerous Amish families, some on foot, most in buggies and wagons, were all headed in the same direction. Cheerful greetings and pleasant exchanges filled the crisp air. Everyone was glad to see a break in the weather.

Sarah declined numerous offers of a ride, content to stretch her legs on such a fine morning. The icy grip of winter would return all too soon.

She turned in at the farm lane where dozens of buggies were lined up on the hillside just south of the barn. The horses, most still wearing their harnesses, were tied up along the fence, content to munch on the hay spread in front of them or simply doze in the sunshine until they were needed to carry their owners home.

The bulk of the activity was focused around the barn. Men were busy unloading backless seats from the large, gray, boxlike bench wagon that was used to transport the benches from home to home for the services held every other Sunday. Bishop Zook was supervising the unloading. When the wagon was empty, he spoke with his two ministers, and they approached the house.

Sarah entered the farmhouse ahead of them. Inside, it was a beehive of activity as the women and young girls arranged food on counters and tables. Most of the small children were being watched over by their elder sisters or cousins. The young boys were outside playing a game of tag.

Catching sight of her aunt Emma visiting with her daughter-in-law Faith, Ada Kaufman and Mary Shetler, Sarah crossed the room toward them and handed over her basket of food. *"Guder mariye."*

"Good morning, Sarah," her aunt replied. "Isn't the weather wonderful?"

"It is." Turning to Mary, Sarah grinned at the child she held, "Goodness, how this little girl is growing. May I hold her?"

"Of course." Mary handed the baby over with a timid smile.

Sarah took Hannah, enjoying the feel of a baby in her arms. Mary's life had not been easy, but did she know how blessed she truly was?

Ada said, "She should be growing. She eats like a little

piglet." There was nothing but love in her aged eyes as she gazed at her adopted granddaughter. Ada had opened her home and her heart to the once wayward Amish girl and her baby.

Emma said, "I see the bishop and ministers coming. We'd best hurry and join the others in the barn."

As she spoke, Bishop Zook and the ministers entered the house and went upstairs where they would discuss the preaching that was to be done that morning. The three-hour-long service would be preached from memory alone. No one was permitted the use of notes. Each man had to speak as God moved him.

Sarah handed the baby back to Mary. The women quickly finished their tasks and left the house.

The barn was already filled with people sitting quietly on rows of backless wooden benches with the women on one side of the aisle and men on the other side. Tarps had been hung over ropes stretched between upright timbers to cordon off an area for the service. Behind them, the sounds of cattle and horses could be heard. The south-facing doors were open to catch what warmth the sunshine could provide.

Sarah took her place among the married women. Beside her, Katie Sutter sat with her three small children, the youngest, Roy, born four months ago. Rachel, the oldest, only four years old, slipped off the bench and crossed the aisle to sit on her father's lap. The remaining child, little Ira began to pout and fuss at his sister's desertion.

Katie slipped a string of beads and buttons from her pocket. She handed them to her little one. He was then content and played quietly with his toy.

From the men's side of the aisle, the song leader announced the hymn. There was a wave of rustling and activity as people open their thick black songbooks. The

*Ausbund* contained the words of all the hymns but no musical scores. The songs were sung from memory and had been passed down through countless generations. They were sung slowly and in unison by people opening their hearts and minds to receive God's presence without the distraction of musical instruments. The slow cadence allowed everyone to focus on the meaning of the words.

At the end of the first hymn, Sarah took a moment to glance toward the men's side. She spotted Levi sitting just behind the married men. His brothers sat near the back. The twins were chewing gum and looking bored. Sarah considered asking Katie if she had any additional toys. In truth, the twins were not the only teenagers looking restless. Levi, on the other hand, held his songbook with a look of intense devotion on his face.

He glanced in her direction, and she smiled at him. He immediately looked away and she felt the pinch of his rejection. Why was it that he turned her every overture aside?

The song leader announced the second hymn. *O Gott Vater, wir Loben Dich* (Oh God the Father, we praise You). It was always the second hymn of an Amish service. Sarah forgot about Levi and his brothers as she joined the entire congregation in singing God's praise, asking that He allow the ministers to speak His teachings, and praying that the people present would receive His words and take them into their hearts.

At the end of the second hymn, the ministers and Bishop Zook came in and hung their hats on pegs set in the wall. That was the signal that the preaching would now begin. Sarah tried to listen closely to what was being said, but she found her mind wandering to the subject of Levi and who might make him a good wife.

Covertly, she studied the single women in the congregation. She quickly ruled many out as being too old or too young to suit him. It would be wonderful if Mary were older, for Levi would make her a strong and steady husband, but she was only sixteen. One by one, Sarah weighed the pros and cons of the remaining women. She ended up with the same women she had considered the day before. Sally, Leah and Fannie.

Confident that one of them would be right for Levi, she focused her attention on the sermon once again.

Levi sat up straight and unobtrusively stretched his back. He was stiff after sitting for nearly three hours. The wooden benches were not made for comfort. At least he hadn't fallen asleep the way Elam Sutter was doing. After Elam's daughter had moved back to her mother's side, the basket maker started nodding in front of Levi. When Elam began to tip sideways, Levi reached up and caught his arm before he tumbled off his seat.

Elam jerked awake. *"Danki,"* he whispered as he gave Levi a sheepish grin.

Levi ventured a guess. "Working late?"

Elam shook his head. "Teething baby."

He leaned forward to look toward the women. Following his gaze, Levi saw Elam's wife sitting across the aisle. Katie Sutter was sitting up straight with her baby sleeping sweetly in her arms. Her face lit with an expression of pure happiness when she caught her husband's glance. Sarah sat beside her.

What Levi wouldn't give to see Sarah look at him with such light in her eyes.

He quickly focused on his hymnal. Such daydreaming was foolishness.

Elam sat back and rubbed his face. He whispered to Levi, "I'm a sorry husband if I can't stay awake to thank God for all the wondrous gifts He has given me."

"I reckon God understands. Our Lord must have been a teething babe at one time, don't you think?"

Elam grinned and nodded. The minister who wasn't preaching at the moment cast a disapproving glare in their direction. They both fell silent. Twenty minutes later, the bishop stopped speaking, and the song leader called out the number of the final hymn. Levi ventured a look in Sarah's direction. She held her songbook open for Elam's daughter Rachel seated beside her. She pointed out the words as she sang them.

Sarah should have children of her own. She would make a good mother. He couldn't imagine why God had chosen not to bless her and Jonas with a baby. It didn't seem right.

The song drew to a close at last. The twins were up and out the doors the second it ended. Teenage boys were expected to sit at the back. Levi always thought that was so their late arrivals and quick getaways didn't disrupt others. He followed more slowly. His eyes were drawn to Sarah as she walked toward the farmhouse with the other women.

How much of his life had been spent watching her from afar, wishing for something that could never happen? Years.

Once she wed Jonas, Levi realized he would have to leave Hope Springs or grow bitter watching Jonas enjoy the happiness denied him. His dream of going to Colorado provided Levi with a goal. He embraced the idea. Only, he had waited too long.

What if Sarah never remarried? How much more of his life was he prepared to give up because of his promise to a dead man?

Sarah joined the women in the kitchen as they prepared the noonday meal while the men rearranged the wooden benches and stacked them to create tables. The majority of the congregation would eat out in the barn, but the bishop and many of the elders would be served inside the house where it was warmer.

Sarah positioned herself beside her aunt, slicing loaves of homemade bread into thick slices. "*Aenti* Emma, I have need of your assistance."

"Anything, child. What can I do for you?"

"I need some help with matchmaking."

Emma looked up with a wide grin. "Has some fine man finally caught your eye?"

"*Nee,* it is not a match for myself. I have a friend who needs a wife. How do I go about getting him to spend time with a possible mate?"

Emma scrutinized Sarah's face. "Is this someone I know?"

"I would rather not say."

"Now I'm intrigued," Emma said, reaching for a second loaf to begin slicing.

"I don't want either party to feel they are being pressured into a relationship."

"In that case, you must find something they have in common or give them each a task that requires the help of the other person."

Sarah looked over and saw Fannie Nissley enter the room. "Aunt, do you know if Fannie is seeing someone?"

Emma looked around to see who might be listening and then leaned closer. "She and Elijah Miller have been keeping company all summer. I expect her father will make an announcement soon."

Sarah crossed Fannie off her list. Just then, Sally Yoder approached the table and put down a box.

Sally said, "I've made a dozen peach pies. Here is the first half if you'd like to slice them. I'll bring in the rest."

Peach pie was Levi's favorite. It was like a sign from the Almighty. Sarah laid her knife aside and said quickly, "Sally, let me give you a hand."

## Chapter Six

Levi stood near a group of men all about his own age. The majority of them wore beards indicating their married status. The recently harsh weather and the price of hay and grain dominated the conversation. Levi didn't farm, and the price of feed meant little other than it would cost more to keep his horses over the winter.

Like many of the Amish who no longer lived on the farm, he kept two buggy horses in a small stable behind his house. Soon, the twins would start asking for courting buggies and high-stepping trotters. He wouldn't begrudge them the cost even though the money would come out of his bank account. Money he'd worked hard to save so that he might one day buy his own shop in far away Colorado.

He had always assumed his family members would be content to move with him, but now he wasn't so sure. Was Grace really ready to marry? If the boys started courting, would they want to leave Hope Springs?

He was surprised out of his musings when Sarah spoke beside him. "Levi, will you help us carry in some of the food?"

Sally Yoder stood slightly behind Sarah. He didn't mind leaving the men, for he was rarely more than an onlooker in the group. He nodded and followed them toward the buggies lined up along the lane.

At the fourth one, Sally stopped and opened the back door. He accepted a large cardboard box from her. She picked up a smaller one.

"Be careful with that, Levi," Sarah cautioned. "It's full of peach pies that Sally baked herself. Peach is Levi's favorite kind of pie. Did you know that, Sally?"

"I didn't." Sally gave her a puzzled glance.

Sarah smiled. "You two go back to the house. I'll be along in a moment."

When they were out of earshot, Sally said, "I could've managed on my own, Levi. I don't know why Sarah thought I needed help."

"I don't mind," he mumbled.

*"Danki."* She blushed as she glanced at him.

She was a pretty girl with bright red hair, fair skin and a dusting of freckles across her nose. She was about the same age as Grace, but he didn't know her well. He couldn't think of anything to say. He was glad to be doing something useful, but the box wasn't heavy. Sally was right. She could've carried it easily.

He glanced over his shoulder. Sarah was still standing by the buggy with a satisfied grin on her face. When she saw him looking, her grin vanished. She immediately started walking toward the barn. He couldn't shake the feeling that she was up to something, but he had no idea what.

At the house, he handed over his box of goodies and started back toward the group of men. He caught sight of the twins sitting on the corral fence, talking to a group of boys about their own age. Not far away stood a group of girls casting coy looks in the direction of the boys.

His brothers would spend most of the day visiting with

their friends. After the noon meal, games of volleyball, horseshoes or other diversions would get underway since the weather was nice. Tonight, there would be a singing, a get-together for the teenagers and unmarried young adults. Levi was happy to consider himself past the age of joining such pursuits. He hadn't enjoyed them even when he was younger. He never felt as if he fit in.

He rejoined the men and listened to the conversation with half an ear. His thoughts kept turning back to Sarah. It wasn't long before she approached him again.

"Levi, would you do me a favor? Leah Belier thinks there is something wrong with her buggy. Would you mind taking a look at it for her?"

He gave Sarah a funny look. This was definitely odd. She seemed determined to see that he stayed busy. "Can't she bring it by the shop tomorrow?"

"No, silly, she has to teach school, and it's too far for her to walk in this weather."

Since the day was bright and sunny he raised an eyebrow. Sarah clasped her hands together and smiled at him. He decided to let her comment slide. "All right. I'll take a look."

"*Goot.* Wait here, and I'll get Leah."

She entered the house and came out a few moments later with Leah in tow. She smiled at the schoolteacher as she said, "Levi would like to take a look at your buggy."

"My buggy? Why?" Leah stared at him in surprise.

"Because you told me it didn't feel right when you were driving it."

"I said it doesn't drive like it did when it was new."

Sarah beamed at her. "Well, Levi's the perfect person to examine it. You don't want to break down on the road, do you?"

"Of course not."

Sarah stopped beside Levi so Leah stopped, too. Sarah took a step back and shooed her along with her hands. "Go on. Levi will check out your carriage and then we can have lunch together when it's our turn to eat."

Levi and Leah exchanged puzzled glances. Levi started walking toward the buggies lined up on the hillside, and Leah fell into step beside him. She said, "Thank you for doing this."

"Sure."

She glanced over her shoulder. "Is it just me, or is Sarah acting a bit strange today?"

"It's not just you."

"I heard that the fabric shop is closed for the winter. Maybe she's feeling lost without her job. I know I would."

"But you must give it up someday."

"Only if I marry. I don't expect that will happen anytime soon."

"Why do you say that?" He studied her intently, wondering why she, like Sarah, seemed to have no interest in marriage.

She blushed and said, "There are many younger and prettier girls in Hope Springs for the men to choose from. I have accepted the fact that I won't have children of my own, so I will continue to teach and love each of my students. I didn't see Grace this morning. I hope she isn't ill?"

"She's gone to visit our grandmother in Pennsylvania."

"Oh, how nice."

Nice for Grace, not for him.

Leah said, "I would love to travel. I've always had a desire to go out West and see the Rocky Mountains."

He looked at her in surprise. "So have I."

"Really?" Her smile brightened.

"I have second cousins who live near Mont Vista, Colorado."

"I've read about the Amish settlements out there. I think it must be wonderful and yet frightening to move so far away. I might like to visit, but I'm not sure I would like to stay. What about you?"

"I plan to move there one day."

"Do you? I'm sure many people in Hope Springs will be sorry to see you go."

Not that many, he thought. Not as long as there was a carriage maker and wheelwright to take his place.

By this time they had reached her buggy. He checked it over carefully. Leah stood with her arms crossed beneath the black shawl she wore over her dark blue dress. She finally broke the growing silence. "Is there anything seriously wrong with it?"

"Your back axle is bent."

"Will it be expensive to replace? Can you straighten it?" she asked.

"It would be better to replace it. I can't tell what it needs until I spend some time under there. Bring it by the shop this week."

"*Danki,* Levi. Is it safe to drive until school lets out Friday afternoon? That way I can leave it overnight."

"Can't say for sure. Have someone follow you home today."

"I will, but I must get to school on Monday and someone can't follow me all week."

She'd done so much for the community over the years. Here was his chance to do something in return. "I'll come by and give you a ride to school and look at your buggy while you're teaching. If it isn't safe, I'll leave one of my used buggies for you to drive until I can fix it."

"That would be much appreciated. I'm glad Sarah thought of this because I wouldn't have had it looked at until it broke down."

"Even a well-built carriage needs maintenance."

"I expect that's true. How are the twins? There was never a dull day when they were my students. I haven't had to check my lunchbox for frogs in two years."

"I'm sorry they were such trouble."

Her eyes narrowed. "I've always wanted to know how they got that skunk into the coatroom without getting sprayed themselves. The school smelled for weeks."

Levi ducked his head. He'd had plenty of notes from Leah about his brothers' behavior over the years. His talks with them hadn't improved their actions. He often wondered how his parents would have handled the boys. He was a sorry replacement for their father.

Leah said, "I'm sure the boys will straighten out."

"Do you think so?"

"It may take a few years. Most rowdy boys get their come-uppance when they become fathers and are blessed with children just like themselves."

"Those boys as parents? God help us all."

Leah smiled. "It is a prayer I utter often. Thank you for checking my buggy."

He said, "I'll see you tomorrow."

She left and returned to the house.

Levi rejoined the group of men beside the barn. When it was his turn to eat, he entered the house and filled his plate. Sarah was at the serving table. With a bright smile, she dished him a large slice of the peach pie.

"Sally Yoder made this one. It's absolutely delicious. She is one woman who knows her way around the kitchen."

Levi accepted Sarah's offering and moved away. He spared one backward glance. She was watching him intently. Something was definitely not right. He didn't have long to think about it because Bishop Zook sought him out.

The bishop said, "I didn't see Grace this morning. I hope she's okay."

"She has gone to visit a relative in Pennsylvania."

Bishop Zook chuckled. "That explains why my son has been moping around the house these past few days."

Levi had no idea what to say so he kept silent.

"I think it will be a good match, don't you?" The bishop looked at him hopefully.

"Haven't given it much thought. Grace is mighty young."

"Ah, but she is old enough to know her own mind. I just wanted you to know that I approve of my son's choice." The bishop winked and walked away.

Levi's appetite deserted him. Was he the only one who hadn't seen how serious Henry and Grace were becoming? He wasn't prepared for his sister to marry and leave home. He wasn't sure he could manage without her.

"Is something the matter, Levi?" Sarah asked.

He hadn't been aware of her approach. "*Nee,* why do you ask?"

"I saw you talking with Bishop Zook. Was it about Grace?"

"*Ja.* He said he approved of the match."

"That is good to know."

"She's too young."

"There are younger wives and mothers here. Why don't you join me for lunch?"

He normally ate with his family, but since the twins were nowhere in sight, he nodded his acceptance.

"Wonderful. Sally and Leah have saved us a place outside."

His spirits dropped a notch. He should've known she didn't want to eat with him alone. That might have started baseless gossip about them.

Leah and Sally were sitting on the open tailgate of a farm wagon. They scooted over to make room for Sarah. Levi held her plate until she got settled. Instead of making them crowd together, he chose to stand beside the wagon.

Leah said, "I was just telling Sally about your plans, Levi."

"What plans?" Sarah glanced between Levi and the schoolteacher.

"Levi is planning to move to Colorado. I think it sounds like a wonderful adventure."

For an instant, Levi was sorry he'd mentioned his desire to Leah, but he reconsidered that thought as he studied Sarah's face. She would have to find out some day. What did she think of the idea?

Sarah managed to swallow the fried chicken she was chewing without choking. She stared at Levi in disbelief. "I didn't know you planned to leave Hope Springs."

"It's nothing definite, but I'll do it one day. Don't worry. You'll be able to rent the business to someone else. Perhaps for more money."

Leah began chatting about the Colorado settlement and its proximity to a wildlife refuge where whooping cranes gathered on their annual migration. Sally was full of questions about the place. Leah tried to include Levi, but to Sarah's chagrin, he kept his focus on his plate.

Sarah gave up trying to listen. She had no idea Levi planned to move away. He was as much a part of her life as the house she lived in and the business Jonas had built.

Levi had always been there. She need only mention to Grace that she was low on firewood and the next morning Levi was stacking a cord of wood along the side of her house. If her horse began limping, Levi showed up to check the animal's shoes and feet for problems. If the business needed upgrades, he came to her with a list of what was needed, how much it would cost and where she could buy what they needed. She had taken his presence for granted. It was hard to imagine life without Levi next door.

"What do you think of the idea, Sarah?" Leah asked.

Sarah realized everyone was looking at her. "I'm sure it doesn't make any difference to Levi what I think."

Leah frowned. "I was asking what you think about having a winter picnic out at my place?"

Sarah felt a blush heat her cheeks. "Sorry, I guess I wasn't listening."

Sally said, "We can have a bonfire and roast hot dogs and marshmallows. We would have to make sure there is plenty of hot chocolate to keep everyone warm."

"I think it sounds like a wonderful idea," Sarah agreed.

"When will it take place? Can we make it a Christmas party on the fifteenth?" Sally asked.

Leah shook her head. "I'll be busy with the school Christmas program until the nineteenth. Let's make it Saturday the twenty-second. I'll need help getting things ready the day before. Levi, would you be able to help me set up some straw bales for seats and boards for tables?"

"I reckon I could."

"Wonderful." Leah beamed at him.

Sarah sat back with a self-satisfied smile. She couldn't have planned that better if it had been her own idea. She took a bite of the mashed potatoes on her plate. If Levi took a wife, he might be much more reluctant to move away.

Sally asked, "Sarah, are you coming to the quilting bee for Ina Stultz? It will be at our home."

"*Ja,* I told Grace I would come in her place."

"We should have a good turn out. Her *mamm* has so much to do with two weddings this year that I offered to host the bee."

"That was very kind of you, Sally. Wasn't it, Levi?" Sarah glanced from Sally to Levi. This was his chance to say something flattering to the girl about her thoughtfulness. He nodded and kept eating. Sarah rolled her eyes.

For the rest of the meal, Sarah studied Levi's reaction to her two friends. His polite response to their questions was usually a monosyllable reply, but neither of the women let that stop them from including him in the conversation. Sarah couldn't detect any interest on Levi's part for either woman. He finished his plate and made his escape, much to Sarah's dismay.

Sally said, "He doesn't say much, does he?"

"He's the strong, silent type," Leah answered.

Sarah quickly added, "He's a hard worker, he's a kind neighbor and a nice-looking man. A woman could do much worse for a husband."

Leah grinned. "Sarah, I didn't know you were on the look out for a *mann*. Levi would be a fine choice for you."

"For me?" Sarah squeaked. She shook her head violently. "I'm not looking for a husband. I was talking about some other woman."

"Sure." Sally winked at Leah.

Sarah saw her plans blowing up in her face. If these women thought she had her eye on Levi, they wouldn't go out with him.

She lowered her gaze and spoke with quiet sincerity. "Levi is a fine man and would make a wonderful husband, but I'm not planning to marry again. No one could replace Jonas. I was simply making conversation."

Sally laid a hand on her arm. "We're sorry to tease you."

Sarah smiled. "I forgive you, but I must ask a favor in return."

"Ask away," Sally replied.

"I need help. I'm taking Grace's place at the carriage

shop while she is gone. I'm supposed to do the inventory this week. I simply can't do it alone. Levi and the twins are much too busy to help me. Could you spare a day or two to give me a hand?"

Sally grinned. "Absolutely. We aren't that busy at Elam's shop now that the tourist season is over. I'm sure he can spare me for a few days."

"I would be more grateful than you know." Sarah took a bite of the peach pie on her plate, satisfied that things were back on the right track. Sally really did make a good pie. Surely, Levi had noticed that.

Levi stayed at the Nissley farm until late afternoon. He enjoyed watching Atlee and Moses play several games of volleyball. Unlike their older brother, the twins were outgoing and well-liked by their peers. They never had trouble fitting in.

When it grew late, Levi helped Eli Imhoff and a few others load the seats back inside the bench wagon. When he finished, he went looking for his brothers. He found the twins waiting for him by the front porch. He said, "It's time to go."

"We were thinking of staying for the singing. We'll walk home later," Atlee said.

Both boys had their eyes focused on a group of young people gathered at the side of the barn. Levi noticed the pretty Miller sisters glancing frequently in his brothers' direction. The girls were twins and the same age as his brothers. Levi accepted that he was on his own for the short drive home.

He fetched his horse from among the few still remaining and backed Homer between the shafts of his buggy. When he finished harnessing the gelding, he turned to get in and found Sarah once again at his side.

"I hate to be a bother, Levi, but is there any way you can give me a lift home? I walked this morning, but it feels like I have a blister forming on my heel. I really would appreciate a ride."

Sarah had never gone out of her way to spend time with him. What was going on? "*Ja,* I can give you a lift."

She got in without waiting for him. He climbed in after her. The inside of his vehicle had never felt so small. Their knees were almost touching.

He swallowed hard and slapped the reins to get the horse moving. As they rolled down the lane, he wondered what he should say.

Sarah had no difficulty talking. "It was a very nice sermon today. Bishop Zook has a way with words that makes you feel that God is speaking through him."

"I reckon He is."

"You're right. Did you enjoy Sally Yoder's peach pie?"

"*Ja.*"

"I knew you would. Peach is your favorite, isn't it?"

"*Ja.*"

"I remember that because it's my favorite as well. Sally is a very nice girl, isn't she? Not a girl really, she's a young woman. Certainly old enough to be courting."

"Nice enough, I reckon."

"Leah Belier is another nice woman. Did you enjoy your conversation with her?"

He slanted a glance at Sarah. "She wanted to know how the twins got the skunk into the coatroom at the school without getting sprayed themselves."

Sarah laughed out loud. It was a delightful sound and made him smile, too. She said, "It was a mean trick, but it was pretty funny. I doubt anyone will be able to top that anytime soon."

"For Leah's sake, I hope not."

"I have to wonder if she isn't ready to give up teaching and get married. She would certainly make a good wife. We all know she has a way with children. Don't you think she would make someone a fine wife?"

"I reckon."

After a long moment, she asked, "Have you thought about it?"

"Thought about what?"

"Honestly, Levi, what have we been talking about?"

"Peach pies and skunks?"

"You are being deliberately obtuse."

"You've been talking about Sally and Leah."

"And if Leah might be ready to wed. Have you thought about marriage?"

He didn't care for the topic. "Have you?" he countered.

She grew somber. "No."

"Why not?"

She stared at her hands. "Because I'll never find someone as special as my Jonas."

It wasn't what he hoped she would say, but one thing Levi knew for certain. He wasn't anyone special.

## Chapter Seven

Sarah counted the number of lynchpins in the wooden box and added the total to the sheet of paper on the clipboard beside her. Inventory was tedious work whether she did it at the fabric store or here. It was part and parcel of a business. It had to be done.

It was her second day of working with Levi since riding home with him after the preaching. She could count on one hand the number of words he'd spoken to her since that evening.

"If he gets past ten words, I can make a tally sheet for him and keep it on my clipboard," she muttered to herself.

The twins were outside working on the church district's bench wagon. Eli Imhoff had brought it in that morning. The rear axle had cracked and needed to be replaced. Fortunately, Levi had an axle that would work and gave the project to the twins to finish before the day was done.

The wagon would be needed to carry the benches to Samuel Stultz's farm for a wedding service the day after tomorrow. The first of his five daughters was getting married. A second daughter, Ina, would be wed in three weeks' time. Sarah had promised Grace she would attend the quilting bee for her early next week. Weddings were wonderful events, but they were also sad reminders of what God had taken away from her.

Through the closed window, Sarah could hear the sounds of the twins' heated debate as they disagreed over the best way to undertake the bench wagon repair. It reminded her so much of the conversations she'd had with her sister when they had been teenagers. Her mother used to say they fought like cats and dogs. Sarah knew that wasn't entirely true. She had loved her sister unconditionally, even if she didn't always approve of Bethany's actions or her choices. She had loved Bethany and God had taken her, too.

If she never loved anyone else, she would never have to suffer such loss again. It was the main reason she wouldn't consider marrying again.

Suddenly, Sarah caught the mention of Leah Belier and she listened more closely.

"He did not," Moses said

"He did," Atlee insisted.

"Levi took Leah Belier, the teacher, riding in his buggy?"

"I saw them together yesterday with my own eyes. What do you think it means?"

"Nothing. It doesn't mean nothing."

Atlee said, "It doesn't mean anything. Have you forgotten all your English classes with Leah?"

"I try to. Give me a hand with this wheel or get lost."

The boys continued to quarrel, but they had given Sarah something to think about. So Levi had taken Leah for a ride. That was promising.

Letting her mind wander for a minute, Sarah shifted her gaze from the twins to where Levi was affixing a new tongue to a farm wagon. In spite of the cool temperature in the building, he had his sleeves rolled up. His light blue shirt was darkened with sweat between his shoulder blades. He was hatless, and she could see the beads of perspiration clinging to the hair at his temples.

He lifted the heavy wooden bar with an ease that surprised her. When he finally had it seated to his satisfaction, he stood back, dusted his hands together and propped them at his hips.

Why hadn't she noticed before what a fine figure of a man he was? While he wasn't a brawny fellow like her husband had been, his slender frame was well muscled. All in all, Levi was an attractive man. She hoped the women she had in mind for him would notice.

Sarah tipped her head slightly as she studied him. She already knew his crystal-clear blue eyes were his best features. His forehead was broad, and his chin jutted out slightly, giving him a look of determination. His nose was a little big for his face, but not overly so. She smiled. He could have been blessed with his grandfather Reuben's nose. Fortunately, he hadn't been.

He didn't smile often, but she knew there was a dimple in his right cheek. It made him look less severe, less aloof. He didn't smile enough.

Sarah was ashamed to realize how much she had ignored Jonas's friend over the past few years. Now that Grace had brought Levi's needs to her attention, Sarah was determined to find him a wife. Her aunt Emma might think he was destined to be an old boy, but Sarah didn't believe it.

She had a plan to change that, and she'd already set it in motion. Levi deserved someone who cared about him, who could work beside him and bear his children to carry on his business.

She stopped when she realized how much that sounded like the hopes she once held dear. It wasn't to be for her.

She shook off the sad thought. Because that dream

wasn't what God had planned for her didn't mean it couldn't come true for Levi and his wife.

A buggy pulled up outside. Glancing out the window, Sarah grinned. Part two of her plan was about to get underway. Sally Yoder stepped down from her carriage.

Sarah hurried to hold open the door for her. "*Guder mariye,* Sally. I'm so glad you could come."

"Good morning, Sarah. I hope I'm not late."

"Not at all."

"Isn't this the strangest weather we're having? Cold and snow one week, sunny and warm the next."

"I'll take sunny and warm any day."

Sally shook her head. "I like snow during the holiday season. Not a lot, just enough to make everything look sparkling and new."

Sarah kept her opinion of snow to herself. She glanced in Levi's direction and found he was watching them. Taking Sally by the elbow, Sarah led her toward him.

"Levi, I forgot to mention that I asked Sally Yoder to give me a hand with the inventory. You don't mind if she helps, do you?"

"I reckon not."

Sarah thrust her clipboard into his hands. "Wonderful. If you have a few minutes, can you show her what needs to be done? I would appreciate it. I've got something on the stove I have to check on. I'll be right back."

She hurried out the front door leaving the two of them together.

Levi had never considered Sarah a flighty woman until she had started working with him. He vowed to be less critical of Grace when she returned. Sally stood waiting for his instructions.

He handed her the clipboard without meeting her gaze.

"This is a list of things to be counted. The shelves and bins are labeled. Write down the number of items you find in each one."

Sally glanced at the clipboard. "That's it?"

"That's it." He nodded and returned to work on the farm wagon.

"Levi, what is an axle nut?" Sally asked as she stood looking at the eight-foot-tall wooden cabinet filled with drawers that covered the west wall.

He put aside the hardware meant to hold the tongue to the front axle and crossed the room to show her the correct drawer. Pulling it open, he said, "It's used to hold the wheel on the axle."

"I thought as much." She counted the ones in the drawer and pushed it closed.

"Anything else?" he asked.

"No, I've got this." She opened a second drawer and began counting.

Levi returned to wrestling with the wagon waiting to be finished.

"Why do you have left and right axle nuts?"

He exhaled in frustration. "Because the nut on the axle had to be threaded to turn right on one side and left on the other side."

"Why?"

"To prevent the nut from being spun off when the wheel is going in the same direction. If that happens, the wheel falls off." He lay down to tighten the bolts under the tongue.

"I see. What is a clip bar used for?"

He finished tightening the bolts, wiped the sweat from his face and rose to walk past to her. "Moses will be in to help you. I have work to do outside."

He rolled down his sleeves, donned his jacket and escaped out the door. How many questions could one woman ask? Outside, he found young Ben Lapp unloading a wheel from his wagon. Ben was a few years older than the twins. He rolled the wheel toward Levi. "I've got a broken fellow on this one. Any chance I can get it replaced today?"

Behind Ben's wagon, Daniel Hershberger was helping his new wife out of their buggy. He had a second horse tied on behind.

Atlee and Moses came hurrying up. Moses took the wheel from Ben. "We can't get to it today. It will be tomorrow afternoon at the earliest."

Ben nodded. "That will work. I also need a new left axle nut."

Levi pointed over his shoulder. "Sally Yoder can find you one."

Ben's eyes brightened. He looked with interest toward the building. "I didn't know Sally was working here." He headed inside without another word.

Dan Hershberger, with his bride, Susan, at his side, approached Levi. They made an imposing pair for both were tall with ample figures and stern expressions. Dan said, "I understand my wife's new carriage is done."

Levi nodded. Atlee said, "I'll hitch your horse for you. The two of you can take it for a ride around the block to make sure it's to your satisfaction."

Susan folded her arms and gave Levi a stern glare, ignoring the twins completely. "I would prefer that my husband harness the horse."

She wisely didn't trust his brothers. Neither of the boys looked disappointed, so perhaps they didn't have a prank in mind. Levi said, "It's this way."

Levi walked toward the back lot. Dan followed, leading his spare horse. It was a high-stepping and spirited coal-black mare. Glancing over his shoulder, Levi saw

Susan waiting near their buggy. She was keeping a close eye on the twins.

The open carriage was sitting in the center of the back lot. Dan's stern face broke into a wide grin when he saw it. "This is exactly what I had in mind. Susan will love it. I hope she will love it, for a happy wife makes a happy life."

The two men hitched up the horse and led her to the front of the building. Susan walked around the buggy, tested the doors, and ran her hand over the leather upholstery. Turning to her husband, she finally smiled. "It is wonderful, *danki, mie* husband."

"It is my joy to see you happy." He opened the carriage door and assisted her to climb in.

Levi happened to catch a glimpse of Atlee's gleeful face from the corner of his eye. A cold feeling settled in his bones. What had they done?

Sarah finished her cup of coffee and took the blue enameled pot off the stove. She hadn't lied. She did have something on the stove—her coffee pot. Glancing at the clock, she wondered if twenty minutes was enough time to leave Sally and Levi alone. Hopefully, he had spoken more than a handful of words to her.

Sarah was anxious to see how the couple was getting along. She rinsed her cup and set it to dry on the side of the sink. When she opened the front door, she saw Dan and Susan Hershberger sitting in their new carriage. Levi was with them and not with Sally. Sarah scowled. She hadn't taken into account that they might have customers.

As Sarah descended her steps, Dan tipped his hat in her direction. Susan lifted her hand to wave as Dan slapped the reins against the rump of his horse. The mare surged forward. Sarah heard a sharp crack. Dan and Susan both fell backward as their seat gave way. The mare trotted smartly down the street with her passengers' legs sticking in the air.

Horrified, Sarah dashed out her front gate. Levi was already in hot pursuit of the couple. Moses and Atlee were clinging to each other as they laughed hysterically. Sarah stopped in front of them. "Oh, how could you?"

"They are such a pompous pair," Atlee managed to say when he caught his breath.

"Ah, Levi's got their horse already," Moses said with a pout.

Sarah looked down the street and pressed her hand to her heart in relief. "Thank heavens. What if the horse had run into traffic or upset the buggy?"

Moses shrugged. "Nothing bad happened. I was hoping they'd go clear through town that way."

Sarah wanted to box his ears. "We're lucky they didn't. Dan Hershberger could buy and sell this business ten times over. He is an influential man. If he decides to make trouble for us, we could lose most of our business."

Atlee said, "He won't make trouble for you, Sarah. You're a widow. The church elders would never stand for that. Here they come. We better get out of here."

The boys took off, leaving Sarah and Levi to face their irate customers alone.

It was an ugly scene. It took the better part of half an hour to soothe Dan and his wife's ruffled feathers. Sarah ended up letting them have their carriage at cost. Levi promised to deliver it to their home tomorrow after thoroughly inspecting it. When they finally left, Levi and Sarah turned to face each other.

"Where did they go?" he asked in a tired voice.

She knew he was talking about his brothers. "They took off running toward the center of town. God only knows where they are by now."

"I can't believe they pulled this off. I knew they were up to something, but if I can't trust them to work for me, what will I do with them?"

"Send them to work for someone else," Sarah suggested.

He thrust his hands in his pockets and stared at his feet. "Who would have them?"

"Your grandfather perhaps?"

"Maybe. I will speak to him."

The silence stretched between them. Sarah glanced at Levi just as he looked at her. She couldn't hold back a grin. "It was kind of funny."

Levi's hangdog expression changed to a reluctant smile that tugged at the corner of his mouth. "*Ja,* it was. Susan Hershberger wears pink bloomers."

"She does?" Sarah choked on a chuckle. Their eyes met. The ridiculousness of the prank hit them at the same time. They both started laughing.

"Snap, wee!" Sarah threw her hands in the air. Levi laughed harder. Sarah pressed her hands to her face as tears blurred her vision.

"Stop," Levi begged her, holding his sides.

"Snap, wee! Pink I see!" Unable to stand because she was laughing so hard, she fell against Levi and grasped his arm. His hands came up to steady her. She looked at his smiling face and her mirth slowly died away.

Their eyes met. Sarah realized that she was practically in his arms. She took a quick step back. His hands dropped to his sides.

She said, "It was funny, but it could've been so much worse."

Levi nodded. His gaze once more dropped to his feet. "Reckon I should get back to work."

"As should I. I have left Sally alone for too long."

"I forgot. Ben Lapp needed a part. Sally must be having trouble finding it for him."

"I'll take care of it." She took another step back but discovered she was reluctant to leave him. The frown had returned to his face. She knew he was once again thinking about his brothers.

"Levi, would you like me to ask Bishop Zook to have a talk with the boys?"

"Do you think it would help?"

"It can't hurt."

"I will speak to him about them. They are my responsibility."

"And none of mine. I understand." She gave a half-hearted, embarrassed smile and hurried toward the carriage shop front door. She heard him call her name. She stopped and glanced back.

He said, "I'm grateful for your counsel."

Her heart grew light again. "I only want to help."

She pulled open the door and went inside. She found Ben Lapp leaning against the counter. Sally stood on the other side, smiling at him as she said, "The right hub nut is threaded to the right and the left hub nut is threaded to the left so they won't spin off the wheel while it's turning."

"For only working here one day you sure seem to know a lot about the equipment."

Sally blushed a becoming shade of pink. "I try to pay attention. Some people think I ask a lot of questions, but it's only because I want to learn new things."

Sarah walked behind the counter with Sally. "And I'm sure that Levi was happy to answer all your questions."

"Actually, he didn't seem happy to answer any of them. Ben helped me finish the inventory of the tall cabinets. He's been wonderfully patient with me." She smiled sweetly at him.

He shrugged off her compliment. "It was no trouble. What are you doing for Christmas, Sally?"

"*Mamm* is cooking a big dinner for the family on Thursday. We have cousins coming from Kilbuck to visit for the long weekend. What about you?"

"That's funny because my folks and I are traveling to my uncle Wayne's place. My grandparents live with his family. His farm is down near Kilbuck. My family goes there and your family comes here."

The young pair were so focused on each other that Sarah began to feel invisible. "Ben, Levi said you needed a part. What can I get for you?"

Sally answered her. "He needed a left hub nut. I found it for him, but I didn't know how much to charge. We've just been waiting for you or Levi to come back."

Sarah rang up the amount on the cash register. "I'm sorry to have kept you waiting, Ben. There was a problem with the Hershbergers' buggy."

"I didn't mind." He hadn't taken his eyes off of Sally.

"Are you staying in Kilbuck long?" she asked.

"Just until Friday evening."

"That means you'll be back in time for the barn party on Saturday." Sally spoke with a nonchalance that was a dead giveaway his answer was important.

"I'll be back in plenty of time. Who's having a hoedown?"

"There's going to be one at Ezra Bowman's farm. Maybe you could come by for a while."

Sarah looked at Sally in surprise. "I thought that was the night of Leah Belier's winter picnic?"

Sally shrugged. "It is. I didn't hear about the hoedown until last night. It should be loads more fun than an old picnic. Leah will understand if I don't come."

A troubled look crossed Ben's face. "Ezra Bowman belongs to the Sparkler gang, doesn't he? Do you run with that crowd? I hear they're a pretty wild bunch."

Sally raised one eyebrow. "We're not goody-goodies, but you shouldn't judge us without getting to know us. Some of them are kind of wild, but most them are like me. Ordinary Amish kids just looking to enjoy their *rumspringa*."

Ben pulled out his wallet and handed Sarah the money he owed. "I'll think about it. It could be fun."

"It will be."

His smile returned. "Okay. I'll see you there and maybe I'll see you tomorrow when I come back for my wheel."

"I'll be here," she said brightly.

When he left, Sally turned and grasped Sarah's arm, bubbling over with excitement. "I can't believe Ben Lapp actually spent the better part of an hour talking to me. He's so fine."

Sarah saw her hopes for a match between Sally and Levi going out the window. She wasn't one to give up easily. "Levi is a fine-looking fellow, too. He's hard-working and much more mature than a boy like Ben."

Sally rolled her eyes. "I know he appeals to someone older—like you—but not to someone like me. We should get back to work or we're never going to get finished here."

Sarah picked up the clipboard. Her first serious attempt at matchmaking was a failure, but Sally was right. They still had a lot of work to get done. "We can move to the upholstery room. That has the second largest number of small items."

Sally followed along behind Sarah. "Why is the upholstery room enclosed? None of the other rooms have ceilings over them."

"To keep the dust out of the cloth in there."

"How much cloth do you keep?"

"It depends on how many orders we have. Often, we

have to special-order fabrics, but if we find a good deal on something our customers like, we'll order in bulk."

As they counted needles, threads and bobbins, Sally continued to pelt Sarah with questions. Before long, she realized that working with Sally was more tiring than working alone. Her patience began to wear thin. After another twenty minutes and as many questions, she said, "I can finish up in here. You've been a big help. Why don't you go ahead and go home?"

"It's barely noon. I'm not going to leave you to do this by yourself. I said I could work for two days and two full days is what you will get. Why are the threads arranged according to size and not according to color?"

"Because they are."

Sarah heard the large double doors at the side of the building open. She stepped out of the workroom and saw Levi pulling the Hershberger carriage in. He was struggling with the heavy vehicle and could barely move it. She put down her clipboard and rushed to help him. Together, they were able to pull it inside.

*"Danki,"* he said and blew out a long breath.

"You should have called me to help. It's too heavy for you to manage alone."

"Don't scold. I thought I could do it." He raised his fist to his mouth and coughed sharply.

Concern sharpened her tone. "You deserve a good scold. If you don't take care of yourself, who will?"

"Grace is normally here to help, but someone told her to take a vacation. Oh, wait, that was you."

"You're not going to start harping on that again, are you? What's done is done."

"Gee, you two sound like an old married couple," Sally said from the upholstery room doorway.

Levi scowled. "I reckon a wife would not talk to me like I was a child."

"Sometimes you act like a child," Sarah said quickly.

"As do you," he snapped back.

Sarah's mouth dropped open. She shut it and marched back into the workroom without another word. Sally moved out of her way. "Sorry."

"That's quite all right. Where were we?"

"Nylon thread, size eight."

Sarah opened the bin. "Four spools."

Consulting the clipboard, Sally said, "Cotton thread, size eight."

"Six spools."

"Are you sure you aren't upset with me?"

Sarah closed her eyes. "I'm not upset with you."

She wasn't upset with Sally. She was upset with herself for promising Grace she would try and find a wife for Levi. She had no business being a matchmaker. She didn't know the first thing about helping people fall in love.

Sally said, "I've learned so much today. Plus, I had the chance to make an impression on Ben Lapp. I've been hoping for a chance to do that for ages, and he'll be back tomorrow."

Her comment gave Sarah pause. Maybe she'd been going about this the wrong way. It might not be about who she thought Levi would like. It could be she needed to find out who liked Levi.

"Sally, earlier you said Levi was attractive to someone who was…older. Were you thinking of someone specific?"

"I shouldn't have said you were older. You're not old."

"Never mind that. Were you thinking of someone else?"

"You have to promise you won't tell her I said anything."

"I promise. Who is it?"

"My cousin Joann."

Joann Yoder? The one woman Sarah had crossed off her list as being too shy. On second thought, the spinster might be the perfect woman after all. She wasn't likely to speak to Levi like he was a child even when he acted like one.

How could she get them together?

"I don't know your cousin very well. What is she like?"

"Quiet, shy, but she has a heart of gold."

That sounded familiar. "What kind of things does she enjoy doing?"

"Joann? She likes to garden and she loves quilting. She's coming to Ina Stultz's quilting bee. You're coming, right?"

"I am." Sarah couldn't envision a way to get Levi involved in quilting.

"*Goot.* Joann likes to cook. She likes to visit. Oh, and she really likes to fish. Yuck. I hate handling worms, but she doesn't mind. She goes with my brothers when they have time."

"She likes fishing? That's very interesting." Sarah smiled. Levi used to go fishing with Jonas. Could he be persuaded to toss a line in with Joann? How?

Sally's eyebrows shot up. "Do you like fishing?"

"It can be…rewarding. I love the taste of fresh trout." As long as she didn't have to clean it before she cooked it.

She would have to get up a fishing trip of her own. If all went well, using Levi Beachy as bait might just land him the perfect mate.

## Chapter Eight

"I know that silly thing is in here somewhere." A crash followed Sarah's muffled words.

Levi, splitting kindling in her backyard, stopped swinging his ax and glanced toward her back porch. It was late in the day and they had finished at the shop an hour ago. The sound of something heavy hitting the floor made him put his tool down. "Sarah, are you okay?"

"I would be if I could just find that rod. Do you know where it is?"

Puzzled, he walked toward the building. He stepped inside and saw Sarah down on her hands and knees pulling out baskets and boxes from beneath a wooden storage bench. "What kind of rod are you talking about?"

"Jonas's fishing rod. I know I still have it. It has to be here somewhere."

"Why are you looking for his rod?"

"Because I'm going fishing."

It was the last thing he expected her to say. "You hate fishing."

She glared up at him. She had a smudge on one cheek and a look of steely determination in her eyes. "I don't hate fishing. I simply didn't like it as much as Jonas did.

Which was why I was always glad he went with you. Why can't I find his rod?"

Levi arched one eyebrow. "I distinctly remember hearing you tell him you wouldn't go fishing until God started making fish that weren't slimy and didn't stink."

She turned back to searching under bench. "I must have been having a bad day."

Levi stepped past her and lifted a four-foot-long black tube off a nail on the back wall. He handed it to her. "Is this what you're looking for?"

She glanced at it and shook her head. "No. I'm looking for a red fiberglass rod with a silver reel thing on it."

He opened the end of the tube and pulled out two rods. One was a dark blue fly fishing rod and the other one was a red spin-casting rod. They had been taken apart to let them fit inside. "I bought Jonas this case after one of my brothers stepped on his favorite rod and broke it."

She rose to her feet looking sheepish and adorable. *"Danki."*

*"Du bischt wilkumm."* He handed them to her.

She took them from him and looked them over. "The pieces just fit together, right? Where are the hooks?"

"In the tackle box you threw aside."

"Oh." She looked at the mess on the floor.

"Are you really going fishing?"

"I can see it may be a more complex undertaking that I first imagined, but I do intend to go. I have to."

"Why?"

"To be out in the fresh air. To enjoy the glories that are the world God has given us. To be at one with nature."

"I ask again, why are you going fishing?"

She closed the lid of the bench and sat down. "I invited my brother and his family to come for Christmas. Apparently, his son loves to fish. I offered to take my nephew fishing if the weather was nice enough while they were here. It was snowing when I wrote the letter. How was I to know it was going to warm up? I received an answer this morning. They are coming for a visit, and Merle is very excited that he is going fishing with his aunt. Can you give me a few pointers so I don't look like a complete fool?"

"Like how to tell a tackle box from a picnic basket?"

"You enjoy poking fun at me, don't you?"

He folded his arms over his chest and stroked his chin with one hand. "I've never gotten to do it before. *Ja,* it's kind of fun."

"Levi, will you take me fishing or not?"

How could he deny her anything? "All right."

"When?" she demanded eagerly.

"Tomorrow?"

"It can't be tomorrow. I'm going to a quilting bee."

"That's just as well. I need to deliver Susan Hershberger's repaired buggy. How about the day after tomorrow?" He had plenty of work to do, but the prospect of spending an afternoon alone at the lake with Sarah was too tempting to pass up.

"I think the day after tomorrow will be fine, but I'll have to let you know tomorrow for sure. What time would we leave?"

"I'll pick you up at one o'clock."

"Where will we go?"

"Down to the old stone quarry. I think the bass fishing will be good there."

Sarah grinned. "It sounds like a wonderful time."

She looked so excited and happy that his heart gave a funny little skip. He never imagined she would be thrilled to spend time in his company.

She went inside the house and he returned to the woodpile. Picking up his ax, he began whistling as he worked.

* * *

Over a dozen buggies and two-wheeled carts lined the lane leading up to Sally Yoder's home. Sally herself greeted Sarah at the front door. "Come in and welcome. Nearly everyone is here except the bride and her family."

"She'll be here." Sarah remembered how excited and nervous she had been at her own quilting frolic, for she knew she and her new husband would spend many nights together beneath the quilt she had designed and pieced together. She had chosen the Birds in the Air pattern in shades of blue, soft creams and bright greens. That quilt was packed away now, for she couldn't bear to sleep beneath it alone.

Inside Sally's home, twelve women were already seated around the large kitchen table. The air was filled with lively chatter. The mouthwatering smells of fresh coffee, warm donuts and freshly made cinnamon rolls added to the party atmosphere.

Sally's father and three of her brothers were setting out straight-backed and folding chairs around the edges of a large quilting frame in the front room. The furniture in the room had all been pushed against the walls to make room. Sunlight streamed in through the south-facing windows. The quilt top was a beautiful Sunshine and Shadows pattern with blocks in shades of blue, green, magenta, pink and violet alternating with rows of black. She wondered what had made Ina choose this particular pattern and fabrics.

Sarah scanned the faces of the women who ranged in age from seventeen to seventy. They were all women she knew well. Nettie Imhoff and her daughter-in-law Katie Sutter were talking to Karen, Nettie's stepdaughter, who had recently wed Jonathan Dresher. Faith Lapp and Rebecca Troyer sat beside Naomi Wadler. Esther Zook, the bishop's wife, was locked in deep conversation with Susan Hershberger. They darted compassionate glances in Sarah's direction.

No doubt, the bishop's wife was getting an earful about the Beachy brothers. Poor Grace would have her work cut out winning over Henry's mother when she came home.

Looking for Joann Yoder, Sarah spied her standing alone near the back door and staring with longing out the window. She was dressed in a drab gray dress with a black apron. Her hair was mousy brown beneath her black *kapp.* Her shoes were coated with drying mud.

After accepting a cup of coffee, Sarah moved to stand near her. "I almost wish it were rainy and dreary out today."

Joann looked at her in surprise. "Why?"

"It's such a beautiful day, cool but not chilly, with plenty of sunshine to tempt a person away from the chores inside. After all, how many more nice days can we expect this late in December?"

"Not many, but a quilting bee is not really a chore." Joann lowered her gaze again, as if she was afraid she'd said too much.

She reminded Sarah so much of Levi that she wanted to give the woman a hug. Not that Sarah was tempted to hug Levi. That wouldn't be proper. Okay, she did feel the urge to hug him sometimes, but only because he worked too hard and his family didn't appreciate all he did.

Sarah said, "You're right, a quilting frolic is much more than stitching. We'll hear familiar tales from the grandmothers, and catch up on their grandchildren's antics. Perhaps we'll even hear some of the latest gossip. We'll sing and laugh together. Later, there would be oodles of food. I can smell the ham cooking already, can't you? The only thing better than this would be a day spent fishing."

*For you and Levi, not for me.*

Joann looked up with interest. "You enjoy fishing?"

Sarah couldn't outright lie to her. She decided to side-step that comment. This was for Levi. She forced a smile and said brightly, "*Enjoy* is hardly the word I would use. My husband took me when we were first married. I never seemed to have time after I started working at the fabric store."

"I know what you mean. I don't get to go as often as I would like, either."

This was her opening. Sarah tried not to sound too eager. "Levi Beachy is taking me over to the old quarry tomorrow. Would you like to join us?"

A look of delight filled Joann's eyes, but it quickly died away. "I'm sure the two of you would rather go alone."

"Not at all. You would be doing me a great favor by join-ing us. Levi is a much better fisherman than I am. I know he'd enjoy the company of someone who isn't a novice."

"Do you really think so?" The fearful hope in her words fueled Sarah's determination. Here was a woman who didn't need to be convinced of Levi's good traits. She just needed a way for him to notice her.

Sarah laid a hand on Joann's arm. "He'll be thrilled. Please say you can come."

"Well, if you're sure it's okay."

"Perfect. We're meeting at my house at one o'clock. Levi said the bass fishing should be good over at the old quarry."

"After this nice warm-up, I reckon it will be. I hooked into a big one there a month ago, but it broke my line. I'm ready to try and land him again."

Sarah felt a sudden pang of envy. Joann and Levi might find they had many things in common besides fishing. That was the reason Sarah had suggested the outing. So why did the look of anticipation on Joann's face leave her feeling jealous?

Sarah faced the true cause of her discontent. She wanted to feel that rush of attraction again. She wanted her heart to skip a beat when the name of a certain someone was mentioned.

Such thoughts were pure foolishness. God had given her the best possible husband, but for some reason, she didn't deserve to know years of happiness with him. The fault lay in her, not in her husband, she was sure of that. Joann and Levi deserved a chance at the happiness that eluded her.

Joann asked, "What's the matter? You look so sad."

Sarah managed a smile as she shook her head. "It's nothing."

The front door opened and Ina Stultz came in with her mother and both her grandmothers. Sarah went to say hello, glad for something else to think about.

Now that the bride-to-be had arrived, Sally's mother invited everyone to find a place at the quilting frame. With so many eager hands, Sarah knew the project would be finished by day's end. She followed the others into the front room and took a seat beside Joann.

Out came the inch-and-a-half-long quilting needles, called "sharps" or "betweens" and spools of thread. For a few minutes, the chatter died away as the women got down to work threading their needles and studying the areas to be outlined. The quiet didn't last long.

"Do you remember when I used to make a play fort under your quilting frame?" Ina asked her mother.

"I do. It wasn't until you were ten that you decided to watch me quilt while you stood beside me instead of playing at my feet."

"Does this quilt have a story?" Rebecca asked, running her hand over the colorful pattern.

Ina smiled. "My mother and her mother both used the Sunlight and Shadow pattern for their wedding quilts."

"To remind us that our lives will be filled with both gladness and sorrow, but that the comfort of the Lord will always be over us," her grandmother explained.

There were murmurs of agreement from around the room.

"From the time I first started setting stitches I wanted to become as good as my grandmother." Ina smiled at her family.

Sarah nodded. Hand-quilting was a journey of personal accomplishment for each Amish girl. Like Ina, Sarah had spent years striving for consistent lengths, working to make straighter lines and improve her stitch count.

For Sarah, her personal best became ten stitches per inch. A goal few quilters could reach. But then, most Amish girls married and began raising families—work that took them away from their craft until their children were grown and they had more time again. Without a husband or children to care for, Sarah had been free to devote her evenings to quilting. She often made two a year. Naomi Wadler sold them for her to the tourists who stayed at the Wadler Inn.

Sarah chose a starting place on Ina's quilt and began to rock her needle through the three layers of fabric stretched on the frame, the solid backing, the batting in the middle to make the quilt fluffy and warm and the top sheet, which bore the pattern. By rocking the needle back and forth, she was able to load as many stitches as possible before drawing the thread through the layers.

Looking up from her work, she saw smiles on the happy faces around her. These women had come together to do something for one of their own. It was a wonderful feeling to join them, young and old alike, as they worked on a craft they all loved.

The skill levels were diverse in such a large group. It was one reason that quilts done at a bee were kept by the families and not offered for sale. Having been employed by an Englishwoman and having met many of the English tourists who came to the store, Sarah knew they prized uniformity in the stitching of the quilts they came to purchase. Such quilts were usually done by one woman.

Joann leaned close. "Watch, Sally will start a contest soon to see who can make the shortest stitches."

Sarah looked over the women. "Anyone who can beat Rebecca Troyer will deserve a prize. You may be a contender. You have a very neat hand at this."

"*Danki,* but my skills are nothing compared to Rebecca's," Joann said.

Rebecca was a renowned quilter in the community. She once suffered from a disease that gradually robbed her of her sight. She had supported herself and her aged aunt by making quilts to sell. With the help of many, and Gideon Troyer in particular, the community had raised enough money for Rebecca to undergo surgery to restore her sight.

By the grace of God, she could now see as well as anyone, but she still kept her eyes closed when she was quilting. She said the sight of so many colors and shapes distracted her from the feel of her needle.

The afternoon passed quickly and Sarah enjoyed the company of her friends. It was getting late when Naomi Wadler spoke up. "Sarah, lead us in a song. Your voice is so sweet."

"Sing 'In the Sweet By and By,'" Ina said quickly.

Closing her eyes, Sarah began, *"There's a land that is fairer than day, And by faith we can see it afar; For the Father waits over the way, To prepare us a dwelling place there."*

Everyone joined in the hymn's refrain. *"In the sweet by and by, We shall meet on that beautiful shore; In the sweet by and by, We shall meet on that beautiful shore."*

When the song was finished, Ina said, "Choose another one, Sarah. What is your favorite?"

Levi trudged along the highway with his horse walking behind him. He was on his way back to Hope Springs after delivering the repaired carriage to Daniel Hershberger's farm. Having driven it over with his own mare, Levi now led his docile Dotty along the edge of the roadway. A few cars zipped past, but the mare kept her head down and walked quietly beside him. The steady *clip-clop* of her hooves on the blacktop provided a soothing sound to their walk.

He'd made one other stop before dropping off the buggy. He had stopped at Bishop Zook's farm. He'd had a long talk with the bishop. He felt his brothers would benefit from the minister's wisdom.

It was late in the afternoon now and the air was growing chilly. The newspaper that morning said to expect two more days of sunshine before the cold weather returned. It looked as if the weather would stay fine for their fishing trip, if Sarah decided she could join him.

Throughout the day, he'd had a hard time keeping his mind on his work. Thoughts of spending a quiet afternoon alone with Sarah kept intruding. He was eager for this day to end and for tomorrow to arrive.

As he crested a hill, he noticed a line of buggies in the lane of the house off to right. He recognized Sarah's gray gelding hitched to the white rail fence.

Dotty lifted her head and whinnied a greeting. Several of the buggy horses replied in kind including Sarah's gray.

He patted Dotty's neck. "Must be the quilting bee Sarah spoke about."

He hoped she was having a good time with the other women. She didn't get out much except to go to work and church and occasionally visit her family. Since Jonas's death, the joy had gone out of her eyes. Levi knew several widows who had remarried and found happiness again. Why hadn't Sarah? Was her grief so deep?

As he passed by the lane, he heard the sounds of singing coming from inside the house. Someone must have opened a window. It was an old hymn, one he particularly liked called, "Savior Like a Shepherd Lead Us."

He stopped to listen. Dotty dropped her head and snatched a bite of grass growing along the roadside. Levi recognized Sarah's pure, clear voice leading the song. He stayed where he was, listening to the words that stirred his soul and embodied his faith until the last note died away.

Sarah had beauty inside and out. What would it be like to have such a woman as a wife? He couldn't imagine the joy that must have been Jonas's.

Levi settled his hat firmly on his head and started walking again. More and more, he found he couldn't stop thinking about Sarah, about her smile and her laugh, about the way she scolded his brothers and put the shop to rights. Tomorrow, he prayed he would see her smile and maybe even laugh, not at him, but with him.

The urge to sing overtook him but he settled for quietly whistling the hymn Sarah had been singing. Tomorrow couldn't come soon enough.

## Chapter Nine

Levi left the shop at noon and went home to eat a hasty lunch. Sarah had stopped by the previous evening to say she could go fishing with him. He didn't want to keep her waiting, but there was one thing he had to do first.

The twins came in to eat a short time later. They had been making wheel spokes and were covered with wood shavings from the lathe. They'd been a quiet pair following the incident with Daniel's buggy. It wouldn't last. He knew they'd be up to something else before long.

He said, "I'm going fishing today. You will stay and run the shop while I'm gone."

The boys looked at each other. Moses said, "We'd like to go fishing, too."

"I would have liked to be paid for the work I put into Daniel Hershberger's carriage. Thanks to you, I labored for nothing."

Scowling, Moses said, "You shouldn't have agreed to give it to him at cost. It's not like he can't afford it."

"Sarah made the offer, and I had to agree to it. She is the owner of the shop we work in. I think you forget that sometimes. The place is not ours to do with as we will."

"How can we forget it? The sign says Wyse Buggy Shop

in big letters." Moses had a mulish expression on his face that troubled Levi.

He said, "I like a good joke as well as the next fellow, but you two crossed the line this time. Someone could have been hurt."

"No one was," Atlee countered, looking chastised.

"No one was—this time. It pains me to say this, but I'm giving you both two weeks' notice. You will have to find jobs elsewhere."

"What?" They gaped at him in disbelief.

"If I cannot trust you to keep the safety of our customers foremost in your minds, you can't work for me. You are free to seek employment elsewhere."

Atlee said, "You can't run the place by yourself."

"I will hire a man I can trust. Perhaps working for someone other than your brother will teach you to value the work you do."

"You mean you're going to stop paying us? How will we get our spending money?"

"That is no longer my problem."

Moses said, "It's not that easy to find a job. Who will hire us both?"

Levi didn't want to punish his brothers, but he had ignored his responsibilities toward them for far too long. He wasn't their father, but he was an adult who knew right from wrong. It was past time they learned a hard lesson.

He gathered his pole and tackle box from the corner of the room. "Daniel Hershberger is hiring at his furniture factory. I heard he pays good wages."

"Ha, ha," Moses said dryly.

Atlee shoved his hands in his pockets and stared at the floor. "We weren't thinking about needing a job from him. We planned to work with you."

Levi looked from one to the other. "You might want to

consider something other than what's funny when you plan your next prank. There are some openings at the coal mine. They will bus Amish workers in. You could try there. One other thing, Bishop Zook will be by to speak to you both later today. Be here when he arrives. If I hear otherwise, you will be looking for a place to sleep as well as work."

With the uncomfortable confrontation behind him, Levi left the house and walked next door. Sarah stood waiting on the front steps of her house. She wasn't alone. Joann Yoder stood with her, pole and tackle box in hand.

Sarah came toward him with a wide smile. "Levi, look who has agreed to join us."

He nodded in Joann's direction. She blushed a fiery shade of red and stared at her feet. His happy anticipation dropped like a stone in a well. He wasn't going to be alone with Sarah.

"Shall we go?" Sarah asked, looking between the two. He nodded again.

"I'm ready," Joann mumbled.

"We are going to have such a nice time. Levi, I can't thank you enough for taking me. Isn't he kind to take time out of his busy day for us?" Sarah started toward his wagon waiting by the street.

He'd chosen to take it instead of his buggy because they would be going off the road and through a farm field to his favorite fishing spot, an old stone quarry now filled with deep clear water from a natural spring. Besides his fishing gear, he'd put in a pair of folding chairs and two quilts in case the day turned chilly.

Sarah scrambled up onto the wagon seat without waiting for his help and scooted across the seat leaving Joann to sit in the middle. Joann smiled shyly and handed him her pole. She held a large bucket in her other hand.

He put her pole in the back of the wagon and said, "I only have two chairs. I'll get another one."

"Don't bother. I just turn my bucket upside down and sit on it until it's time to take the fish home."

Sarah said, "Isn't she clever, Levi? I never would have thought of that."

He took the bucket from Joann and put it in back. She climbed up onto the seat and he took his place beside her.

As they rolled out of town, he glanced over at Sarah. Joann had her pressed against the far side of the seat. He feared she would be knocked off if they hit a bump. He asked, "You okay?"

Sarah grimaced. "I'm a little crowded. Joann, can you scoot closer to Levi? He doesn't bite."

Joann giggled and slid over.

"A little more, please," Sarah said.

Joann moved closer until her hip was touching his. Did Sarah really need that much room? Their destination began to feel a long ways away.

He said, "Elam Sutter has a nice pond. It's closer than the quarry lake if you'd rather go there?"

Sarah quickly dismissed his suggestion, "The quarry sounds much better, doesn't it, Joann? I've never been there and I'm dying to see it. You've been there before, haven't you Joann?"

Joann nodded but didn't say anything.

After a few minutes of silence, Sarah said, "Joann was telling me that she hooked into a really big bass last month. Tell Levi about it, Joann."

"It broke my line."

"What weight were you using?"

"Five pound test."

"Six would have been better."

"That's what I have on now."

"Should be good enough." He couldn't think of anything else to say so he fell silent.

Sarah had no such problem. She continued to pelt them with questions about fishing and their best catches, what kind of lures they used and what type of fishing they liked best. He began to wonder if she had taken a job writing for a fishing journal. It wasn't until they reached the turn-off for the quarry that she finally seemed to run out of questions.

The ride across the field was rough, but it was less than a mile to the edge of the quarry. Levi chose a spot with a sloping shoreline exposed to the sun and drew the horse to a halt.

Sarah hopped down. "What a lovely lake. I think I'll explore a little before I start fishing."

She took off at a quick pace along the edge of the water. He got down and raised his arms to help Joann. She blushed scarlet, but allowed him to lift her down. He quickly stepped back.

Brushing at the front of her coat, she glanced up at him and said, "I hope you don't mind my coming along."

"*Nee,* it is fine." She wasn't to blame. He should have known Sarah wasn't interested in spending time alone with him.

Joann scowled. "I didn't realize Sarah was such a chatterbox."

He looked over her head to where Sarah was walking at the water's edge. "She doesn't usually talk your ear off."

Joann cast a worried look in Sarah's direction. "If she keeps it up, she'll scare the fish away."

"Let me get our poles." If he couldn't spend the afternoon alone with Sarah, he might as well try fishing.

Sarah remained some distance from the wagon and covertly watched Levi and Joann. It looked briefly as if they were having a conversation, but they soon parted ways and actually began casting their lines in while standing fifty feet apart. This wasn't going as she had hoped. Now what?

She wandered father away and found a place on a flat rock between a pair of cedar trees. Leaning forward, she propped her elbows on her knees and settled her chin on her hands. Matchmaking was turning out to be much harder than she thought.

She was almost hoarse after carrying a conversation alone for five miles. Between Levi's stilted replies and Joann's brief comments, Sarah had been tempted to knock their heads together.

Reaching down, she picked up a rock and tossed it in the lake. She was about ready to give up. She had been foolish to think matching Levi up with her friends would be a way to avoid the winter depression that normally gripped her. Grace would simply have to find the courage to leave home without a wife for Levi to replace her.

Standing, Sarah picked up a flat rock and tried to skip it across the still surface of the lake. It sank two feet in front of her. She couldn't even skip a stone right, how could she manage someone else's love life?

"Point number one. If you throw rocks at the fish, they won't bite."

Startled, Sarah spun around to see Levi standing behind her.

He held out her casting rod. "You asked for some pointers, remember? Point number two. It helps to actually put your hook in the water."

"Right." She took the rod from him. She thought she remembered how to cast, but when she tried, her lure plunked into the water barely four feet from shore. Was she doomed to be a failure at everything?

Levi stepped closer. "Reel it back in. Let me show you how it's done."

He stood close behind her and wrapped his hand over hers. "Move your arm back like this, and then go forward. Keep your eyes focused on where you want your line to go."

As he moved her arm back and forth, mimicking the motion she needed, Sarah completely lost interest in fishing.

The firmness and warmth of Levi's hand over hers made her breath catch in her chest. He stood only a fraction of an inch behind her. If she leaned back just a little she could rest against him. She closed her eyes.

The urge to lay her head back and melt into his embrace was overpowering. She had been alone too long. She didn't want to be alone anymore.

He stopped moving her arm. She was afraid to open her eyes and look at him. What would she see written on his face? Indifference? Friendship? Or something more?

"I've got one!" Joann shouted. "Hurry, bring the net."

Levi stepped away from Sarah. The breath rushed back into her lungs. She trembled, but managed to say, "I've got this. Go help Joann."

As he strode away, Sarah called herself every kind of fool. She wasn't a potential wife for him. Even if she wanted to marry again, which she didn't, he hadn't shown the least bit of interest in her *that* way. He was a friend. She had no business thinking of him in any other light.

For Sarah, the afternoon passed slowly, although Joann and Levi both landed fish. An hour later, Levi landed a huge one. The sight of his excited happy face only made Sarah more aware of how attractive he was.

Joann looked as excited as he was. "It's a beauty, Levi!

I think it's the very one that got away from me last month. What kind of jig are you using?"

"This is a black *Jig and Pig*."

"I'm going to have to get me a few."

"I've got several. Try one of mine."

Joann grinned. Her shyness had evaporated. "That's nice of you, Levi. I believe I will."

Sarah glanced between the two of them. Who would have thought something called a *Jig and Pig* could spark such interest between two people? The more relaxed they became with each other, the worse Sarah felt. Her plan was working, so why wasn't she happy?

Within an hour, they had a stringer loaded with eight fat bass. Sarah had a bite or two, but they got away. Her heart wasn't in the adventure. She wanted to go home and bury herself under the covers until her common sense returned.

She made the long ride home in silence. Joann, on the other hand, spoke with growing confidence. Levi gave his usual short replies, but occasionally expanded them to a full sentence or two. Sarah often felt his gaze on her, but she studiously avoided looking in his direction.

When they arrived back at her home, Levi took the fish to clean them. Joann followed Sarah into the house.

Once they were in the kitchen, Joann grabbed Sarah in a quick, strong hug. Just as quickly, she released Sarah and took a step back. She clasped her hands together. "Sarah, I had such a wonderful time. You can't even know."

"I'm glad." She was. One of them should be happy.

"Levi is such a fine fellow. I've never enjoyed a day fishing more than I enjoyed this one."

"I hope you get to enjoy other days together."

"That would be nice, but I'm not holding my breath."

"Why do you say that? You're good company, you enjoy

many of the things Levi enjoys, I don't see why he wouldn't ask you out again."

Joann looked at her sadly. "Sarah, Levi isn't interested in me. It was exciting to imagine he might be for a while, but I know the signs. I've seen the way my brothers and cousins look at the women they want to court. Levi doesn't look at me that way. He looks at you that way."

Sarah's mouth dropped open. For the most part, Levi ignored her unless the business needed something. She'd lived beside him for years. "You are mistaken. Levi and I are friends, but nothing more."

Joann gave her a quick puzzled look and then stared at her feet. "I'm sorry I said anything. Forgive me."

"There's nothing to forgive."

"I must get home. Thank you again for inviting me." She hurried out the door.

Sarah moved to the window and watched her walk away. Joann was mistaken. Levi didn't harbor the kind of feelings that she suggested. Sarah would have known if that were the case. She would have seen it in his beautiful blue eyes.

She glanced toward his house and saw him standing in the yard. He wasn't watching Joann's retreating figure. His gaze was on Sarah's window, but he was too far away for her to read his expression.

Levi didn't know what he had done wrong, but Sarah wasn't speaking to him.

All day long on Friday, whenever he went in search of her, she was heading away from him. If he went to the upholstery room, she made some excuse about needing another type of thread and took off for her house. She handled the customers easily. She smiled and laughed with them, but when she was alone with him, she suddenly thought of things she needed to do elsewhere.

Twice, he cornered her in the small office, but each time she simply said, "Excuse me," and slipped past him. Short of grabbing her and demanding to know what was wrong, he had no idea what to do.

Not only had Sarah turned cold, so had the weather. A gusty north wind rattled the shutters of the building and low gray clouds blotted out the sky. The nice weather had come to an abrupt end as winter returned. The weather forecast was calling for snow by the end of the week.

At four-thirty, Leah Belier drove up and came inside. Since he hadn't a clue where Sarah had gone, he was forced to leave the new carriage he was finishing and speak to Leah. At least she was easy to talk to. "Good afternoon. Are you ready to leave your buggy with me?"

She smiled. "I am. I have one of my students bringing in the used buggy you loaned me. I see you are building a new one."

"*Ja,* it is almost done."

"Who is it for?"

"This one is for someone who needs one right away."

"Like a family who has lost theirs in an accident?"

"Something like that. It's plain inside, but I can change a few things if someone wants to fancy it up. It's a good all-round buggy for a small family. I try to keep one or two finished samples on hand. This will make number three."

"Can I see it?"

"Sure." He led the way.

"Where is Sarah, today?" Leah asked.

"Around." He wasn't about to try and explain something he didn't understand.

Leah opened the carriage door and looked it. "The upholstery is lovely in this shade of gray. I would only change a few small things."

"Such as?"

"I'd need a bigger storage box added to the back and a cup holder up front. I like to sip my diet soda on the way to school in the mornings. It's my one vice."

"Diet soda isn't much of vice. Mine is fresh orange juice."

She laughed. "Levi, that isn't a vice. Orange juice is good for you. Didn't you learn anything in school?"

"Not enough, I reckon. I didn't have you for a teacher."

"Seriously, would you sell me this buggy? How much is it?"

He named a price and waited, expecting her to decline.

Instead, she said, "I'm tempted. Mine is almost fifteen years old and needs work. If I have to put out the money, I may as well get something I like. But not for as much as you're asking." She named a slightly lower price.

It was a fair offer. He didn't want to turn down a sale, but he wanted to make sure she wasn't doing this on an impulse. "You'd best think it over."

"I have been thinking about it ever since you told me what was wrong with mine. I'm ready to do this." She broke into a wide grin.

Could she really afford new on her teacher's salary? He said, "Why don't you take a look at some of the used carriages I have out back? They won't be as expensive."

"Honestly, Levi, you act like my money is no good."

"I want you to be happy with what you buy from me."

"I'm sure I will be. You haven't forgotten about helping me set up for my winter picnic have you?"

"I haven't. When should I come out?"

"There won't be a lot to do. If you come the evening before, that will be fine."

"It's the weekend before Christmas, is that right? I'll be there."

"Wonderful. I will look at your used buggies, but I'm

afraid only a new one will do now that I've made up my mind."

He led the way to the back door and held it open for her. The twins were outside cleaning the ashes from the fire pit. They both had folded kerchiefs covering their noses and mouths. As Atlee hefted a shovelful of ash into a wheelbarrow, a gust of wind sent a cloud of it swirling toward the shop door.

With a muffled cry, Leah covered her face with her hands and turned into Levi's arms.

Startled, he held still. "What's wrong?"

"There's something in my eye. Oh, it hurts. I think a cinder flew in it."

"Let me see. Hold still." He cupped her chin and turned her face up to his.

Sarah opened the front door of the workshop and looked around for Levi. She wouldn't be able to keep running away from him forever, but she wasn't ready to face him. Not if what Joann suggested was true. It couldn't be.

Yes, their friendship had grown in the past days, but it was only friendship. She wouldn't allow anything else.

It wasn't in her to love a man the way Levi deserved to be loved. To love a man as deeply as she had loved Jonas would mean facing the possibility of loss and grief again.

She couldn't live through another loss. It would be better never to love someone again.

She heard the sound of soft voices and rounded the counter to see if he was working in the back of the building. If he was, she could slip into the office and finish the day in there.

When she spotted Levi near the back door, she couldn't believe her eyes.

He and Leah were locked in an embrace not twenty

feet from her. Levi tenderly cupped Leah's face and bent toward her. Was he going to kiss her?

Shock shook Sarah to her core. She quickly turned away.

Levi wasn't in love with her. He was in love with Leah. Why hadn't she seen it?

Instead of the elation that should have filled her at knowing her plan had worked, all she felt was disappointment. With astonishing clarity, she could imagine herself in Levi's arms, lifting her face to receive his kiss.

She quickly left the building. Outside, she leaned against the door and pressed a hand to her stinging eyes, surprised to find tears on her face.

Sarah squeezed her eyes closed but she couldn't shut out the sight of Leah in Levi's arms. She couldn't ignore the ache growing in her heart. He cared for someone else.

Leah was a lovely woman and a good match for Levi. Perhaps she was a bit too conservative for him, but none of that mattered if Leah truly cared for him. Did she? Or was she a desperate old maid leading him on so she wouldn't have to spend the rest of her life alone?

Sarah shook her head to clear her thinking. Such un-Christian thoughts didn't become her. She'd started her matchmaking project to keep her depression at bay and to help Grace, but now she realized what she really wanted was for Levi to be happy.

To love and be loved in return was one of the most beautiful gifts God could bestow on a man and a woman.

Tears came to her eyes again. Grace and Henry would be happy. Levi and Leah would be happy. Everyone would be happy except her. Why had God chosen this life for her?

No, that was wrong. She mustn't question God's plan for her. Her life was blessed with her remaining family and good friends. She had her health and a church community that would rally around when she needed it.

She would grow old alone. So what? Many women did. If she wasn't content, that was something she would pray to overcome. Pressing the heels of her hands to her eyes, she stemmed the flow of tears. It was better for her to live alone than to suffer the constant fear of losing someone dear.

Wasn't it?

It was the belief she's clung to for years, the reason she refused to consider remarrying. So why did she question that decision now? Because in one moment of weakness she thought she wanted to be kissed? Such foolishness would pass.

She would do her best to be glad for Levi and Leah and pray that they would have many happy years together.

# Chapter Ten

"Good morning, Levi. Isn't it a lovely Monday morning?"

Levi still didn't know what he had done to upset Sarah last week, but it seemed that she had forgiven him. He looked out the window. "It is pouring rain."

"Rain is nice sometimes. I can't believe Christmas will be here in two weeks. This year has flown by. Are you doing anything special for the holidays?"

At least she wasn't avoiding him anymore. He said, "The boys and I have been invited to Gideon and Rebecca's place for dinner next Sunday. I plan to have a quiet Christmas at home. When will your brother and his family arrive?"

"Next Monday evening. They intend to stay here for a few days and then go to visit Emma and her family."

"You should invite them to Leah's winter picnic."

Sarah's smile vanished for just an instant. When it reappeared, it was brighter than before. "That is a wonderful idea, but I'm not sure they will stay the whole week. Were you able to fix Leah's axle?"

"She has decided to buy a new buggy instead."

"Really, I had no idea you were such a good salesman."

Something in her tone made him look at her closely. "Sarah, are you okay?"

"Of course. Why do you ask?"

"No reason, I guess."

"You should get to work. I have plenty to do. I made chicken salad sandwiches for lunch and put them in your refrigerator. Where are the boys?"

"Out looking for new jobs."

"What?" She stared at him in astonishment.

"I had a talk with Bishop Zook. He made some suggestions and I took them. I fired Atlee and Moses. After their stunt with Daniel and Susan's buggy, I can't trust them to work here."

"Wow."

"I'm sorry if you disapprove."

"I'm not saying you're wrong. I'm just surprised."

"Hundreds of people ride in the buggies we make and repair. Many more than that depend on the wheels I've sold them. I take the safety of our people seriously. A faulty wheel, a carelessly tightened bolt could kill or maim. I will hire someone new to help me. Ben Lapp is a good boy. I will see if his father can spare him from the farm this winter."

Her eyes filled with sympathy. "It must have been hard for you to tell the twins they couldn't work with you. They're your family."

"The boys were only two when our parents died. Grace was only six. She became the little mother, but I never became the father. I didn't believe I had the right to take my father's place. They lacked discipline because of that. I pray I have not learned my lesson too late for them to become good and wise men."

She stepped close and laid a hand on his arm. Gazing into his eyes, she said softly, "I am pleased with you, Levi

Beachy. If they become good, wise men, it is because they have a good and wise brother."

He covered her hand with his. "*Danki,* Sarah. You have made me see the error of my ways with them. They will have you to thank, as well."

She snatched her hand away and stepped toward the counter, avoiding his gaze. "I can't believe how quickly this place gets dirty. I must get to work and so must you. I have bread baking in my oven. I'll be back in a little while if that's okay with you."

"Of course."

She quickly went out the door.

Did his touch repulse her? Her rejection stung, but he called himself a fool for expecting otherwise. At least she wasn't laughing at him anymore. Her sympathy for his family dilemma was real.

After replacing the axle on Leah's old buggy, Levi worked at fixing up the inside, tightening the door hinges and adding a new shine to the old leather interior with saddle soap and elbow grease. When he finished, he surveyed his work. He now had a nice used buggy to resell. Maybe to a young couple just starting out who couldn't afford a new one yet or as a runabout for a grandmother to use. He glanced outside. The rain had stopped.

He went to the front of the shop and found Sarah cleaning. Didn't she realize she was never going to get this old building spic-and-span? He didn't like to see her working so hard at something impossible.

He wanted what Jonas had wanted for her. He wanted to see her happy, with her children around her and a man who loved her at her side. Then and only then, Levi could follow his dream.

His eyes were drawn to his calendar. Instead of the

mountains he loved to look upon, a picture of a collie dog with puppies stared back at him.

He rounded on Sarah. "Where's my calendar?"

She stopped cleaning. "I tossed it on the rubbish heap. It was years out of date. I got you a new one."

"If I wanted a new one, I would've gotten it myself." He charged past her and out the back door and stopped in disbelief. Not only had she thrown it on the rubbish heap, but she had set the trash on fire. His calendar was charred beyond recognition.

"I'm sorry," she said from behind him. "I didn't think it was important."

It was only a picture. It held no value to anyone except him. The anger drained out of his body. "I wish you had asked, that's all."

It wasn't his dream going up in smoke. It was only a photograph.

"I'm sorry," she said again. "Why was it so special to you?"

"It was just a pretty place. I liked looking at it."

"That was where you hoped to live one day, wasn't it? Oh, Levi, I am sorry."

"I don't imagine I'll ever leave here. It was a pipe dream, nothing more."

He turned away from the fire. His promise was keeping him here. She was keeping him here. How much longer could he stay? Perhaps it was true that he was never meant to leave. The rain began falling again.

He said, "You should go inside before you catch your death." Without looking back, he crossed the lot to his house and went inside. The twins sat at the kitchen table with sandwiches piled on their plates.

He opened the refrigerator. There wasn't any left for him.

He took out the milk carton and poured himself a glass. Moses said, "We haven't had much luck today."

"Neither have I," Levi mumbled and took a seat at the table with them. He downed the milk and wiped his lips. Atlee pushed half a sandwich toward him.

He nodded his thanks and finished it in two bites.

Moses pulled an envelope from his pocket. "The mail came. You have a letter from Grandmother."

Atlee said, "I hope she's sending Grace home."

Levi did, too. He tore open the letter and began to read his grandmother's spidery handwriting.

"What does she say?" Atlee leaned closer.

"She is thrilled to have Grace with her. Looks like Grace intends to stay until the week after Christmas."

"That's not too long." Atlee didn't look thrilled with the news.

Moses rolled his eyes. "I thought she'd hot-foot it back here to be with Henry."

Levi read the next sentence and stopped. "This can't be right."

"What?" Moses and Atlee asked together.

"I'm to be thankful Grace's friend has agreed to be a matchmaker for me." Levi couldn't believe what he was reading. Grace's friend? Was she referring to Sarah?

Moses took a bite of his sandwich. "Grandmother must be getting senile."

"Reckon so," Levi said, but he kept reading.

*Give somber consideration to each woman that is presented to you. A pretty face does not a good wife make. A woman who is devout, who loves God and keeps His commandments, that is a woman who has a beautiful soul. Love grows from respect and shared experiences. Be kind and receive kindness in return. Love and receive love in return.*

Suddenly, all that had been happening since Grace left began to make sense to Levi. Sarah inviting Sally to work with them. Sarah convincing him Leah wanted him to look over her buggy. Sarah inviting Joann to join their fishing trip.

Sarah *was* matchmaking. Trotting him out like a prized horse for consideration.

As if he couldn't find a wife by himself if he wanted one! He hadn't looked seriously because a wife might not want to move to Colorado if she had family in Ohio.

It had been his father's dream long before it became Levi's. His mother had kept his father from going. She had refused to move one step farther west from her family in Pennsylvania. Levi remembered his father's caution on the subject of choosing the right spouse all too well.

Had Grace suggested this matchmaking scheme? Why? Oh, how Sarah must have laughed. The wretched woman, how could she? Were all her friends in on the joke?

He had waited patiently for Sarah to marry for five long years, and now she was wife-shopping for him?

Well, two could play at matchmaking. If he was fair game, so was she. There were any number of men who would be happy to hear that the pretty widow Sarah Wyse was finally on the lookout for a husband.

She hadn't asked him if he wanted to meet potential wives. He saw no reason to ask her if she wanted to meet potential husbands. When the shoe was on the other foot, she wouldn't be laughing then.

What he needed was a strategy. He couldn't think with his brothers staring at him. "I'm going out."

"But it's raining," Atlee pointed out.

"I've got a hat. A little water won't hurt me."

Sarah couldn't put her finger on what it was, but when Levi came back from lunch, something was different about him. He had a hard look in his eyes when he stared at her. His coat was soaked and his hat was dripping all over her freshly cleaned floor.

He said, "I'm going over to the café. The boys didn't leave me but two bites of a sandwich."

"I can make you some scrambled eggs or a grilled cheese sandwich if you don't want to go that far."

"No, I like the food at the Shoofly Pie Café. I won't be long."

"All right. Have a nice lunch."

He smiled, but it didn't reach his eyes. "It's going to be a fine one. I can feel it in my bones."

She puzzled over his comment, but didn't know what to make of it. He was back a little over an hour later. When he took his coat off, she saw his shirt was damp and he had a smear of what looked like blueberries across the front of it. She said, "It looks like the pie was good, how was the rest of your meal?"

He patted his stomach. "The meal and the company were fine. You have no idea how many men eat lunch at the café."

"Mostly the single ones, I reckon. Those who don't have a wife to cook for them at home."

He grinned and pointed a finger at her. "You are correct."

"You're soaking wet. You should go change."

"I'm a grown man. I'll change my clothes when I'm ready and not before. I'll change my life when I'm ready and not before."

"Levi, you're acting very strange."

"Am I? What could have brought that on?"

"Are you feeling well?"

His grin faded. "*Nee,* I'm not."

"Is there anything I can do?"

"You've done enough, Sarah Wyse. You've done more than enough." He left her and went into the office, closing the door behind him. She was left to puzzle over his behavior for the rest of the afternoon.

The sun came out shortly after one o'clock. When the twins came in, Sarah left them in charge at the counter and took the opportunity to go home and get her wash done. If the rain held off, her clothes would be dry by the time she left work.

She was back at the shop an hour later. The twins were where she had left them. They hadn't done much work at all. When four o'clock rolled around, she tapped on the office door.

"What is it?" Levi asked from inside.

"I'm going home now."

"Fine." He sneezed loudly.

Sarah frowned at the door. Was he upset with her? She hadn't done anything to anger him. Perhaps he and Leah had a quarrel after…after she saw them in each other's arms.

Whatever was wrong, it wouldn't be solved by lurking outside Levi's office. She had plenty of work waiting at home. She had oodles of baking to get done before her family arrived.

As she crossed the street, she noticed rain clouds rolling in again from the north. She rushed inside the house and grabbed a laundry basket, intent on getting her clothes in before the rain undid all the sun's work. She had just started taking down her sheets when the first sprinkles splattered against her *kapp* and face.

From behind her, she heard a man's voice. "Let me give you a hand with these, Sarah."

Startled, she turned to see Jacob Gingerich pulling

clothespins from her pillowcases. "*Danki,* Jacob. What are you doing here?"

"I was passing by and decided to stop in for a visit. How are you?"

She bundled the last of her clothing into a basket and lifted it. "I'm fine. Won't you come inside for some *kaffi?*"

His grin widened. He took the basket from her. "I was hoping you would say that."

His joy seemed out of proportion to her simple offer of coffee. Sarah led the way inside the house.

Jacob Gingerich worked in Daniel Hershberger's lumber mill. He was fairly new to the Hope Springs area, having come from Indiana to find work. He wasn't married, and she knew him only from having seen him at the church services. She could think of no reason for him to be passing by her house because Daniel's mill and the farm where Jacob lived were on the other side of town.

She said, "Just set the basket on the floor and have a seat at the table. It will only take me a few minutes to get some coffee going."

He set the basket down, then hung his coat and his hat on one of the pegs by her front door.

She moved to the sink to fill the coffee pot with fresh water. Looking out, she noticed Andy Bowman getting out of his buggy at her front gate. He had a large paper sack in his hand with the Shoofly Pie Café logo on the front. She looked at Jacob. "Are you expecting Andy Bowman?"

He frowned. "*Nee,* I'm not. Why do you ask?"

"Because he's coming up my front walk." She moved to open the door for him.

"Good afternoon, Sarah Wyse," Andy said in a booming voice.

"Hello, Andy. What brings you here?"

He thrust the paper bag toward her. "I thought you

might enjoy a supper that you didn't have to cook. I had Naomi Wadler pack up some of her fried chicken, potato salad and shoofly pie."

One male visitor was unusual. Two single men showing up at her door unannounced smacked of her aunt Emma's matchmaking meddling.

Sarah opened the door wide. "Come in, Andy. Jacob Gingerich and I were about to have some coffee."

She stepped aside. Andy hung up his coat and hat beside Jacob's. The men scowled at each other briefly, but were cordial to one another.

As it turned out, it was a good thing that Andy had brought food. By suppertime, there were four sets of coats and hats lined up beside her front door. Sarah had no idea what her aunt could have said to bring so many bachelors and widowers to her door, but she planned to give her aunt a stern talking to the next time they met.

Once the sparse meal was done and the second pot of coffee had been finished, her guests still made no move to leave. It seemed that none of them wanted to be the first man out the door. They stayed until Sarah finally had to ask them to leave.

As he left, each man promised to return at a more opportune time when they could be alone. When the last one was out the door, Sarah stood on the porch and watch them disperse. She glanced toward the carriage shop and saw Levi leaning against the open door jamb. He gave her a jaunty wave.

Sarah stepped back inside the house and closed her door with a bang. She considered nailing it shut but decided moving away might be a better option. She should have known her aunt wouldn't wait forever before deciding Sarah had been single long enough.

\* \* \*

Levi suffered a twinge of conscience the following morning when Sarah came to work looking as if she hadn't slept well. Her eyes were puffy and she kept yawning into her hand. He hadn't slept that well, either. Today his throat was raw. He had a burning pain deep in his chest.

He said, "There isn't much work today. Why don't you go home? I'm sure you have a lot to do before your family arrives."

"I have a lot of baking to do, that's for sure. I had hoped to get started last evening, but that didn't happen."

"I noticed your party. I felt a little left out, not being invited and all."

"I didn't issue the invitations, but I'm surprised you didn't get one. When I see my aunt Emma, she is going to get an earful."

So she didn't suspect him. That was good, but he didn't like the idea that she was blaming someone else. Still, like the twins, she had to learn that not everyone could be manipulated for her benefit. He pulled a chair up beside her. "Why are you angry with your aunt?"

"Emma Lapp loves the idea of being a matchmaker. I've told her for years that I'm not ready to marry again. I reckon she decided to take matters into her own hands. Hence, half the single Amish men over twenty-five were grouped around my table last night. No doubt the rest of them will show up tonight."

He stared at his hands. "What makes you so sure your aunt is behind it?"

"I can't imagine who else it would be."

"I sympathize with you, Sarah. I've been feeling like I've been put on display myself, lately."

She frowned. "You have?"

"It's not a comfortable feeling, as I'm sure you noticed."

Her frown turned to a look of speculation. "Levi, do you know something about the line of men in my kitchen last night?"

He folded his arms over his chest. "About as much as you know about fishing lines."

She had the decency to blush. "I did promise my nephew I would take him. Thanks to your help, I'm sure I won't embarrass myself."

"Thanks to Joann you mean. And our special thanks must also go to Sally for all her help with the inventory. Is it done?"

Sarah's voice grew smaller. "Almost."

"What sweet young thing can I expect to help you finish?"

"I'll be able to manage alone," she mumbled, her eyes downcast.

He hid a smile behind the hand he used to rub his chin. "That is *goot*."

He heard a horse stop outside. He glanced out the window. "Ah, I see you have another visitor at your house. I believe that is Amos Fisher. He's a long way past twenty-five, but he runs a nice hog farm. He told me yesterday that he has two hundred sows now."

Her eyes snapped to his, shooting daggers of loathing. "I think you are a sneaky, mean man, Levi Beachy."

He grinned. "I'm learning from the best."

## Chapter Eleven

When Sarah entered the carriage shop the following morning she had every intention of giving Levi a piece of her mind. Three more suitors had darkened her door the previous evening.

She found Levi huddled in front of the stove with his arms wrapped around his body. When he looked up, his face was pale as a sheet. There were dark circles under his eyes. He shivered so violently that he nearly fell from the small stool he was perched on. The man looked sick to death. He coughed and the deep rattle in his chest frightened her.

"Levi Beachy, I never once considered you to be a fool until this moment." She advanced toward him.

"Go away," he muttered in a pitifully hoarse voice.

"You are the one who is going. You're going straight to bed. You look miserable."

"I'm fine. I just need a minute to get warm." He leaned closer to the fire.

Shaking her head, Sarah marched to the door and flipped the Open sign to Closed. Outside, Elam Sutter was just getting out of his buggy. At least she knew he hadn't come to court her. He was happily married to her friend Katie.

She opened the door and called out to him, "I'm sorry Elam, but the shop is closed today. Levi is sick."

"I've stopped by to pick up a part he ordered for me. I had a note in the mail that it had come in."

"All right, I'll find it for you, but you should stay outside. I don't want you taking sickness home to Katie and the *kinder.*"

"*Danki,* Sarah. I'll wait right here."

Closing the door, she quickly checked the counter area but didn't find anything with Elam's name on it. She crossed the room and crouched beside Levi. He was looking worse by the minute. She touched his shoulder gently. "Levi, where is the part that came in for Eli Sutter?"

He opened bloodshot eyes. "On my desk in the back."

"I'll get it, and then you are going back to the house."

"I don't want to go to the house."

"You sound like a pouting child. You're going back to the house if I have to drag you by your suspenders. And don't think for a minute that I can't do it."

A ragged cough followed by a weak nod was her answer. She pulled off her coat and tucked it around his shoulders. He nestled into the warmth with a grateful sigh. Leaving him sitting by the fire, Sarah quickly found the part and carried it out to Elam.

He took it from her and asked, "Is there anything I can do for you or Levi?"

"*Nee.* Rest is what he needs now."

"My mother said a nasty flu bug has been making the rounds over in Sugarcreek. Looks like it's come to pay Hope Springs a visit."

"Levi got soaked yesterday and wouldn't go home to change. I hope it's the flu and not pneumonia. He's too sick to work, but he won't go to bed, either. Sometime men are more trouble than they are worth."

Elam chuckled. "My wife would agree with you."

"Good day, Elam. Give Katie and the children my love."

He promised to do so and drove away. Sarah hurried back inside just as Levi was struggling to his feet. He teetered and would have fallen if she hadn't rushed to hold him up. Staggering under his weight, she managed to keep both of them upright.

"I'm sorry," he mumbled against her *kapp*.

She had both arms around his waist. "Never mind. Let's get you to the house. What on earth possessed you to try and work today?"

"I thought I'd feel better in the shop."

"Why would you think that?"

"I always feel better here. Besides, I have work that must be done."

Sarah lifted Levi's arm and placed it around her shoulder. "The work will still be here tomorrow."

"If I don't get it done today, there will be twice as much work tomorrow."

"Let the twins do some of it."

"They're sick. I told them to stay in bed." So it was an illness that was going around and not because Levi had had a soaking. Still, it certainly hadn't done him any good.

"You told the twins to stay in bed, but you couldn't take your own advice."

A vicious cough stole his breath and left him wheezing and unsteady. She knew if he lost his balance she wouldn't be able to hold him up. Why had she sent Elam Sutter away? He wouldn't have had any trouble carrying Levi.

"Come. It's only a few steps to the house. We can get there together."

Thankfully, they were able to manage the short trek,

although several times she wondered if they would make it. They were both sweating and out of breath by the time they reached his front door.

*"Danki, mie goot Sarah,"* he said as he sank in a heap on the couch.

Why did she wish she were his good Sarah? It wasn't part of her makeup to be a loving wife. Hadn't that been made painfully clear to her?

She unlaced Levi's boots and pulled them off. As she had once suspected, both his socks had holes in them. She would have to have a stern talk with Grace when the girl came home. The art of good housekeeping wasn't reserved solely for a woman's husband.

Sarah pulled a folded quilt from the back of a rocker and spread it across Levi. She coaxed him to give up her coat and then tucked the quilt around his shoulders. She pressed her palm to his forehead. He was burning up.

"If I make you some hot tea will you be able to keep it down?" she asked.

"I think so."

"When was the last time you had something to eat?"

"I'm not hungry. I just want to sleep."

"Not until I get some fluids in you. I'm going to check on the twins."

When Levi didn't respond, Sarah took it as his consent. She quickly put the kettle on and made her way up the narrow stairs to the upper story of the house. The first room she looked into belonged to Grace. It was painted a lovely shade of lavender with a large throw rug on the floor and a beautiful lavender-and-white quilt on the bed.

The next door she opened was to Levi's room. It was tidy and clean. The walls were a pale gray. His bed had a simple dark blue blanket as a spread. He was a tidy man.

The last room she looked in was not neat at all. There

were clothes strewn on the floor, shoes had been tossed aside and lay where they'd fallen and numerous books and magazines lay helter-skelter around the room. From a set of twin beds, one bleary-eyed and one bright-eyed boy looked at her in astonishment. She marched to the bed closest to the door and laid her hand on Atlee's brow.

He was hot, but his fever wasn't as high as Levi's.

Moses drew his covers up to his chin when she came toward him. "What are you doing in here?"

"I'm seeing who is sick and how sick they are." She clapped a hand on his forehead. He was cool to the touch. His eyes were bright, his lips weren't cracked.

She fisted her hands on her hips and glared at him. "You aren't sick."

"I am. I ache all over. My stomach is churning. I feel terrible," he insisted.

"You'll feel better when you're done helping me."

"Helping you do what?"

"Levi is downstairs and he is very sick. I don't think I can get him up to his room by myself. You have five minutes to get dressed, and then I'm coming up here with a pail of cold water. If you're in this bed when I get back, you'll get a bath."

"You wouldn't?"

"Trust me, I would."

She turned to leave. Stopping by Atlee, she straightened his covers and said, "I'll bring you some hot tea with honey in a few minutes. Do you think you can eat something?"

"Maybe some toast if you don't mind making it." He coughed harshly.

"I don't mind a bit. Try and get some rest."

"Yes, ma'am." He closed his red-rimmed eyes with a sigh.

Downstairs, she found the kettle starting to whistle.

She took it off the heat and filled two big mugs with the steaming liquid. She added tea bags and honey, and then set two slices of bread in the oven.

She checked on Levi. He was curled up on the sofa with the quilt pulled tight around his neck.

The poor man, he looked miserable, but there wasn't much she could do for him. "Levi, can you drink some of this?"

He shook his head and burrowed deeper under the quilt. Giving up, she carried the mug back in the kitchen.

Sarah glanced at the clock. When the five minutes was up, she found a saucepan and filled it with cool water. She flipped a towel over her shoulder and set the pan, the tea-filled mug and a plate with the toast on a tray. She carried it all up the stairs. As she suspected, Moses was still in bed, trying to look as if he belonged there.

Setting the tray down on Atlee's nightstand, she helped him sit up in bed by arranging his pillows at his back and gave him the mug of tea. He wrapped his hands around it and took a sip. "*Ach,* that's *wunderbaar,* Sarah. *Danki.*"

"You're welcome." Taking the pan, she walked around his bed and threw the water on Moses.

He came out of the covers yowling like a scalded cat. He stood in his pajamas, glaring at her while water dripped from his hair. She took the towel from her shoulder and held it out. "I couldn't find a pail. You're lucky all I found was a small sauce pan."

He snatched the towel from her. "I'll catch my death for sure now."

"I doubt I'll be so lucky. Get dried off, get changed, strip your bed and clean up this mess. All of this mess." She indicated the rest of the room.

Without waiting for him to reply, she turned toward the door. Atlee sat in his bed with a stunned expression of disbelief on his face. She said gently, "Finish your tea, dear. It will help bring the fever down."

He nodded. She smiled and walked out the door.

Twenty minutes later, Moses came into the kitchen. He was dressed in his work clothes. He held a bundle of sheets in his arms.

She took them from him. "I've made some scrambled eggs and hash browns. When you're finished with breakfast, you can help me get your brother up to his room. I may need to send you for the doctor later, so stay nearby."

He frowned and glanced in the living room. "Is he really that sick?"

"I'm afraid he may be." Her own father had died of pneumonia. His illness had started out the same way as Levi's. She always thought her father's stubborn refusal to see a doctor had contributed to his untimely death.

She wouldn't think about another death at Christmas. God would not do that to her. Besides, she didn't love Levi. There was no reason he might die.

She said, "I don't know if Levi took care of the horses this morning or not. Would you please check and take care of them if he didn't?"

"Will you pour more water on my head if I say no?"

She sighed heavily. "*Nee,* but I will be sorely disappointed for I have always thought you had the makings of a good man in you. I know Levi believes you do, and I trust his judgment."

Moses cast her a sheepish glance and then stared at his boots. "I'll take care of it. Keep my eggs warm, will you?"

"Of course."

He pulled on a coat and settled his hat on his head. When he glanced back at her, she realized how much he looked like Levi. Maybe he would grow into a good man after all. She prayed it would be so.

She spent the next half hour coaxing Levi into taking the cough medicine she found in the bathroom cabinet along with a couple of aspirin and sips of warm sweet tea. She could tell it was an effort for him just to raise his head, but he managed to swallow a full cup of the liquid. She left his side feeling better about his condition. Moses came in as she put the kettle back on.

"The stock is taken care of. I've stoked the fire in the shop. I can finish most of the work that Levi had planned for today. How is he?"

"He took some tea. Do you think we can get him upstairs?"

"It would be easier to bring one of the cots down here and move him onto that."

"That's a good idea, Moses. I'll let you do that while I get the laundry started. I need to get your sheets out on the line so you have someplace dry to sleep tonight."

"I can always sleep in Grace's or Levi's room."

"Won't Atlee feel better knowing you're close by?"

"I reckon you are right about that. I'll go get the cot."

Between the two of them, they got Levi moved to a more comfortable bed close to the fire. It didn't make him happy. He fretted for the next hour, more concerned about Sarah than about his own comfort.

"You must go home, Sarah. I don't want you to become ill because of me."

She tucked his quilt more tightly around him. "I'm a grown woman. I'll go home when I want to and not before."

"I wondered how soon that remark would come back to haunt me."

"Rest and don't worry about me. I feel fine. It is up to God if I catch your flu. Now hush. I will hear no more about leaving. Atlee is sick, too. Who will take care of him with Moses in the shop all day?"

Levi said, "I will see to the boy's needs."

Sarah was tired of arguing with him. She stepped back and raised her hands. "Okay, I was about to take some soup up to him, but you can do it."

"Finally, the woman is minding me. Praise the Lord." He pushed his covers aside and sat up.

When he didn't go any farther, Sarah said, "The soup is in the kitchen."

He teetered on the side of the cot. Closing his eyes, he lay back with a moan. "I can't do it."

"I told you so."

"You're laughing at me. You're always laughing at me," he muttered wearily.

"*Nee,* I have never laughed at you, Levi."

He opened his bloodshot eyes and stared at her. "Yes, you have."

"When?"

He started coughing again. She brought him a drink of water. He took a sip and lay back with his eyes closed.

She should let him sleep, but his comment bothered her. "When did I laugh at you, Levi? If you thought I was, it wasn't on purpose and I'm sorry."

"It was on purpose. You wanted me to kiss you…and then you pushed me in the creek. Everyone saw. Everyone laughed."

She recalled the day vividly. She was saddened to realize he thought she had acted deliberately. She reached down and brushed a lock of hair from his forehead. He needed a haircut. She was pleased to note his skin felt cooler.

"You startled me, Levi. That's why I pushed you away. I didn't mean for you to fall in the water. I'm sorry the others laughed, but I wasn't laughing."

He rolled on his side away from her. "I want to sleep now."

"All right. I'll be here if you need me." He didn't answer.

She left him alone and took a bowl of soup up to Atlee. She was pleased when he managed to eat most of it. She hoped Levi would be able to take some later.

With Moses working in the carriage shop, Sarah got busy on something she had been dying to do for days—putting Levi's house to rights.

She re-washed all the dishes in the cupboards. As she suspected, some of them had had only a cursory cleaning. After that, she scrubbed down the kitchen walls and counters. She was getting ready to mop the floor when she heard the door open. Expecting Moses, she was surprised to see Nettie Imhoff and her aunt Emma coming in.

She rushed to stop them from entering. "There is sickness in the house, ladies. It would be best to visit another time."

Nettie set a large basket on the kitchen table. "My son Elam told me as much. Knowing that Levi is a bachelor, I came to see if I could be of use. I stopped by Emma's place and asked her to join me."

"Men are no good at taking care of themselves or anyone else when they're sick," Emma declared.

"You look like you could use a stout cup of coffee. I can do that much." Nettie untied her bonnet, hung it along with her coat on the peg by the door and smoothed her apron.

"That sounds lovely." Sarah kept her voice low so she wouldn't disturb Levi.

Nettie glanced at the cot in the other room. "How is he?"

"A little better, I think. I was very worried this morning. Atlee is sick, too, but his fever isn't nearly as high as Levi's."

Nettie said, "My friends in Sugarcreek wrote that this

flu has been harsh, but it only lasts a few days. Levi and his brother will be better in no time."

Sarah felt the unexpected sting of tears in her eyes. "I'm silly to fret, but with Christmas coming I can't help but worry that something bad will happen again. Jonas, my parents, Bethany, they were all taken from me at Christmastime."

Emma drew her into a comforting hug. "God has given you far too much grief for one so young, but do not doubt His mercy."

Sarah sniffed and wiped her eyes. "You're right. I must lean on His strength."

"What can we do to help?" Nettie asked.

"Until Levi or Atlee need something, I'm trying to put this house in order."

Emma frowned at the grimy floor. "The house is missing the mistress."

"I can't give Grace high marks in housekeeping. Levi seems to be the only one in the family who likes an orderly existence. The twins are slobs."

The older women chuckled and Sarah smiled. It was good to have them here. She hadn't realized how scared she had been. Having Levi laid up brought back so many bad memories of her husband's illness and death.

"A strong cup of *kaffi* first, then we clean," Emma declared. She glanced toward the living room and lowered her voice. "While the men are stuck in bed and can't mess it up before we're finished."

With the three of them working, they were able to scrub the kitchen floor, strip and air the beds, wash a half dozen loads of laundry and clean the bathroom, all before two-o'clock in the afternoon.

Sarah blew out a weary breath as she hung the last sheet on the line. She glanced down the rows of bed linens, shirts, pants and socks flapping in the breeze. Thankfully, the day was sunny. She'd be able to gather them in a few hours and begin the process of ironing, mending and putting them away. She'd forgotten how much work it was to do laundry for more than one person. She was tired, but in a good way.

At least her string of suitors wouldn't come looking for her over here.

Her aunt and Nettie left after exacting a promise that Sarah would send for them if she became ill or the Beachy brothers didn't recover as expected.

Levi refused any supper, but since he was keeping liquids down, Sarah left it at that. Atlee was feeling better while Moses came in looking worn to the bone. Sarah laid a hand on his forehead. "Are you feeling ill now?"

He shook his head. "It was a busy day, that's all."

"Levi will be pleased when he learns how you stepped in to take his place. I've left some soup on the stove and there is fried chicken staying warm in the oven. Just put the leftovers in the refrigerator."

He sniffed the air. "What's that funny smell?"

Sarah tried not to laugh. "Pine cleaner."

"Oh."

"Moses, I'm sorry about tossing water on you this morning."

He grinned. "I reckon Atlee and me played enough jokes on you that I had a little payback coming. Just remember what I said about pranks."

"It's only funny the first time?"

*"Ja."*

"I'll see you first thing in the morning. Don't be afraid to come get me if either of them get worse." She glanced once more toward Levi's bed. He would be fine. She had to have faith. So why didn't she?

\* \* \*

Levi wasn't sure if he was still among the living, but he decided he must be when he rolled over and every muscle in his body protested.

Daylight streamed in through the window on the east side of the house. What time was it? How long had he been asleep?

He sat up in bed and discovered he could do it without getting dizzy. He was definitely on the mend. Maybe it had been Sarah's tea.

He realized he was thirsty. Rising, he made it as far as the kitchen. There was a pitcher of orange juice and several glasses on the table. He sat down and poured himself a drink. It tasted wonderful.

"You need a haircut." Sarah was standing behind his chair. He should have known she was in the house. When was the last time one of the twins made fresh-squeezed orange juice? Before he could form an answer, she was running her fingers through his hair.

His ability to speak vanished altogether. He stopped breathing. It was the first time a woman who wasn't his sister or his mother had touched him like this.

"I never realized you have such nice curls." She tugged gently, testing the length and thickness of the hair he battled into smooth submission with a brush each morning. His scalp prickled, and gooseflesh rose on his arms. A shiver raced through his body.

She stopped. "Are you cold?"

He wasn't, but he lied. "A little."

"Do you want to move closer to the stove?"

*"Nee."* He could already feel the heat building in his body. Did she realize how her touch affected him? He hoped not. He prayed not.

She said, "How foolish of me. A haircut can wait until you're feeling better."

Even if he had been at death's door it wouldn't have mattered. All he wanted was for her to keep her fingers in his hair. He managed to say, "I reckon a haircut is past due. Might as well get it over with. If you don't mind the chore."

"I don't mind at all. Let me get a towel." She seemed delighted with his capitulation. She left the room humming and returned a few moments later with a large white towel under her arm, scissors and a comb in her other hand.

Setting her tools aside, she shook out the towel and put it around his neck, fastening it behind him with a safety pin. Taking up the comb, she studied him for a moment. He glanced at her from beneath his lashes.

Her blue-green eyes narrowed as she assessed his head. She tilted her face first one way and then another. She ran the comb through his hair. It caught on a tangle and he winced.

"I'm sorry."

"It's all right." He prepared to withstand a few more pulls for his hair was matted from his fever.

She started combing again, more gently. "Levi, can I ask you something?"

*"Ja."*

"Yesterday, you said… Oh, never mind."

"I accused you of laughing at me. I know you weren't. You were only trying to help."

"That's true, but you said when we were in school that I…that I asked you to kiss me. Why did you say that?"

"It was a long time ago. Can we just skip it?"

"I want to know what I did that gave you that impression."

"Impression? You wrote me a note. It said to meet you

by the creek if I wanted to kiss you. What other impression was I going to get?"

She stopped combing his hair. "I did not."

Anger rose in him. "Now you're saying I'm a liar?"

Taking a seat beside him, she faced him without flinching. "I don't know a more honest man than you, Levi Beachy. You must believe me when I say I did not write you such a note."

"If you didn't, why were you waiting under the willow tree?"

Her eyes widened, and she sat back with a stunned expression on her face. "She wouldn't have."

"Who?"

Her eyes narrowed. "Did the note say exactly where I would be?"

His anger drained away. He was tired, and he wanted to lie down again. He didn't want to rehash the most embarrassing event of his youth. "Does it matter?"

"I guess not, but I think I know what happened. My sister was a prankster equal to or better than your brothers. When school let out that day she said she had a surprise for me. I was to wait by the willow tree and keep my eyes closed. Then you came, and I forgot all about her surprise."

Sarah rose to her feet and resumed combing his hair. "I'm sorry she made you a pawn in her game, Levi. Bethany never thought how her actions would affect others."

All this time he had blamed Sarah, and she hadn't had anything to do with his humiliation. What a fool he had been. What a fool he still was. "I'm sorry I fell into her trap so easily."

"We were kids. It happened. It wasn't a bad kiss, you know."

Embarrassment made him want to sink through the floor. Why did she have to admit that now?

She stopped combing and bit the corner of her lower lip. "I need better light."

He started to rise, but she laid a hand on his shoulder. "Just scoot your chair a little closer to the window."

The legs of the chair grated on the wooden floor as he shifted closer to the light. She pressed her hand to his chest to stop his forward movement. "That's fine."

When his poor heart started beating again, Levi realized with a jolt what Gideon had recognized weeks ago.

Levi cared about Sarah. Not just as his responsibility, not because she had been Jonas's wife, but because she was a warm and vibrant woman. As much as he wanted to deny it, his heart would no longer be silent.

He was falling foolishly and hopelessly in love with Sarah, and she treated him like a brother.

She stepped behind him and carefully pulled the comb through his hair again. The rasp of the teeth over his scalp, the tugs when she encountered tangles, none of those small discomforts mattered, because each time she smoothed them away with her other hand. She started humming again.

No matter how he felt, he knew she would never return his feelings. She had loved her husband. Levi was a poor substitute for a man such as Jonas. It was pure foolishness to think anything else.

He would never embarrass her with unwanted displays of affection. He was good at keeping his feelings hidden. He would remain her friend as he had promised Jonas he would.

She ran her fingers through his hair again. "I haven't done this in a while. I hope I remember how. Are you sure you're not too tired to do this?"

If he said yes, she would stop. He should send her

away. He opened his mouth to do so, but couldn't speak the words. Instead, he said, "I'm fine."

She said, "Here goes." He heard the snip of the scissors.

Levi closed his eyes and gave himself up to the forbidden luxury of her touch.

## Chapter Twelve

She was making a terrible mistake.

Sarah knew it even before she began cutting locks of Levi's hair. Her barbering skills were adequate to the task, but what about her self-control?

Her desire to do this small, wifely task had seemed so innocent when it first occurred to her. Now, with her fingers entwined in Levi's curls, she admitted her motives were far from innocent. She wanted more than to run her fingers through his hair. She wanted to know what it would be like to be held in his arms, to be kissed by him.

How had this happened?

In the space of a few weeks she had come to see Levi as much more than the neighbor and friend that he had been for five years. Her plan to uncover the man behind his shy exterior was meant to help her find the right kind of woman for him. The real Levi was a man with a quiet soul, a big heart and a wonderful sense of humor…someone who thrilled her with the simple touch of his hand.

And he was courting her friend, Leah.

That was exactly what she had hoped would happen. Only now, she wanted to undo what she had done. She wanted to keep the man she had uncovered to herself.

How selfish she was. This wasn't about what she wanted anymore. Levi had become more important to her than she ever expected. She cared deeply about him.

She drew the comb through Levi's hair, measuring with her fingers and cutting away the excess. What would he do if she told him how she felt? Probably fall out of his chair. In five years he hadn't given the least hint that he saw her as anything more than his dear friend's widow.

Should she ask him about Leah? It wasn't any of her business.

What if he married Leah and they began happily raising their children next door to her? Could she watch from her kitchen window and not be jealous of their happiness? She wasn't sure.

Would it be better if he moved away? Or would not seeing him be worse? Would he finally follow his dream of living where he could see the Rockies from his front porch each morning? She was torn between praying for his happiness and praying for her own.

She drew his hair upward, snipping the long ends and letting them drop to the towel around his shoulders. She worked slowly, but she was finished all too soon. She plucked one perfectly formed crescent from the towel and slipped it into her pocket. She would keep it as a memento of today.

When he was gone or married, she would be able to remember the texture of his hair beneath her hands and how she longed to press a kiss to his brow.

She stood behind him with her hands resting on his strong shoulders, relishing the feel of his strength beneath her palms.

After a few moments, he asked, "Are you finished?"

His voice was rough and raspy. She chided herself for

keeping him sitting here while she indulged in a sad fantasy. "I'm finished. I didn't give you many bald spots."

"Lucky for me, I get to wear a hat."

She started to turn away, but he captured her hand and held it tight. The air around them became charged with electricity. She stopped breathing, waiting for him to speak.

She heard footsteps on the stairs before he could say anything. One of the boys was coming down. Levi released her hand, and she moved quickly to fetch the broom leaning in the corner of the kitchen.

*"Guder mariye."* Atlee entered the kitchen wearing a threadbare blue robe over his pajamas. His hair was disheveled and he looked tired, but his eyes were bright and his color was better.

"Good morning, Atlee. How are you feeling?" Sarah unpinned the towel from Levi's neck and began sweeping up the loose hair on the floor. She was careful not to meet his gaze. Her stolen time with him was over. She had to come back to the real world.

Atlee sat beside Levi at the table. "I'm a little better. Brother, how are you?"

"I think I'll live."

Sarah cringed at his jest. Life was short and precious and could be snatched away in an instant. *Please, Lord, grant him long full years here on earth before You call him home.*

"Where is Moses?" Levi looked toward the stairs.

Atlee yawned and propped his elbows on the table. "He went out to take care of the stock about an hour ago. I reckon he's working in the shop. Delbert Weaver brought in his buggy late yesterday. His door was snapped clean off when a pickup sideswiped him. Moses is going to put a new one on this morning. Delbert said his son was hurt pretty bad. He might loose his arm."

"Which son?" Sarah asked. They had gone to school with several of Delbert's children.

"Roman. They took him to a hospital in Cleveland."

"How awful." Roman was only a few years younger than Sarah.

Levi shook his head sadly. "He was the star of our school's baseball team and a fine fellow. We must pray for his healing."

It would be a sad Christmas season for someone other than herself. She needed to put her own fears and worries aside and stop being selfish in her grief. "I must see if we can organize a quilt sale to help pay his hospital expenses. I have two quilts I can donate."

Levi smiled at her warmly. "I can't sew, but I can donate a set of wheels."

Atlee said, "We could hold an auction here after Christmas."

Sarah nodded. "What better way to celebrate the great gift God bestowed on mankind than to help someone in need?"

Levi met her gaze. His eyes were filled with an emotion she couldn't read.

Atlee sat up straight. "What's for breakfast, Sarah? My bellybutton and my backbone are getting to be best friends."

Levi dropped his gaze. What would he have said if they had been alone?

"I'll have oatmeal and bacon in a few minutes. Levi, what would you like? Toast? Poached eggs?"

"I reckon I'd like to lay down in my own bed for a bit. Thank you, Sarah, for everything." He smiled at her, but it was a smile tinged with sadness.

When he had gone upstairs, Atlee brushed a loose piece of hair from the tabletop. He had an odd expression on his face. He glanced at her several times, but couldn't seem to find a way to speak his piece.

"Is something on your mind, Atlee?"

"We had a letter from our *grossmammi* the other day."

"Is she enjoying Grace's visit?"

"I reckon. Grace is staying until the week after Christmas. Sarah, you haven't really been matchmaking for Levi, have you?"

Embarrassment flooded her face with heat. "What gave you that idea?"

"Grandma wrote that one of Grace's friends was matchmaking for him. Moses and me thought it might be you."

So that was how Levi found out. She sighed deeply. "I admit I was trying to help, but Levi has no need of a matchmaker."

"Course not. He's not the marrying kind."

"You may be mistaken about that."

"What do you mean? Is Levi is seeing someone?"

"I shouldn't say. When he is ready to wed, he will tell you."

"*Nee.* Who would marry my brother?"

"A very blessed woman, if you ask me."

Sarah suddenly glared at Atlee and shook a finger at him. "You must not play tricks or jokes on them, Atlee. Hearts are not playthings."

He held his hands in the air. "All right. We won't, but it would help if we knew who she was."

"I will not say, but if you open your eyes, you can put two and two together. You know who your sister has been seeing, don't you?"

"That wimp, Henry Zook."

"He is not a wimp. He is your sister's choice. She may wed him one day. You must respect that."

"Okay, but the only woman Levi has been around much is you. Is he courting you?"

An intense sense of loss settled in her chest. "*Nee,* he is not. I believe he has been seeing another."

"Wait, do you mean Leah Belier? The teacher?" His voice shot up an octave.

Perhaps now the boys would realize Levi's life no long revolved around them. "It is for Levi to say, not me. How do you want your oatmeal?"

"Oatmeal is oatmeal." His dejected tone made her smile.

"Not when you add brown sugar and cinnamon or raisins. Would you like to try it?"

"Levi can't be serious about the teacher. That would be awful. If she came to live with us it would be worse that being in school again. She has eyes in the back of her head. She'd make us toe the line day and night."

"Someone should."

He stayed silent, but he wore a belligerent expression that gave her pause.

"I'm sorry I said anything, Atlee. Levi may not be serious about anyone. But if such a thing does happen, you must be happy for him no matter who his choice is."

Sarah noticed a lock of hair against the table leg that had escaped her broom. Leaning down, she plucked it from the floor and added it to the one in her pocket. Tonight, she would press them between sheets of tissue paper and place them in her Bible. Then she would pray for Levi's happiness and not for her own.

Levi made a rapid recovery. Sarah didn't come to his home again after she cut his hair. He would not soon forget those moments together, the feel of her hands, the whisper of her breath, the scent of her body so close to his. It had taken all the willpower he possessed not to take her in his arms and declare his love.

Would she have been repulsed by his actions, or would she have accepted his advances?

He wasn't half the man Jonas had been, but maybe Sarah could love him just a little. She didn't have to love him the way she had loved her husband. He could accept that. He would spend a lifetime trying to make her happy and keep her safe.

He didn't know what answer she might have given him. He lacked the courage to act.

He saw her only briefly the following day when she stopped in at the shop to tell him she wouldn't be able to work until after Christmas.

He understood, but he missed her and found himself spending most of the day looking out the window toward her house. At least two more men dropped by to visit her. Levi's punishment for his little joke was having to watch and wonder what was going on inside her home until each man left. Just because he lacked the courage to declare his feelings didn't mean another man would have such trouble. He prayed for courage and the chance to learn how she felt about him.

On Sunday evening, Levi joined his family at the home of his cousin Rebecca and her husband, Gideon. His grandfather Reuben and Reuben's wife were there, as well. Levi's grandmother died before he was born. Lydia was his grandfather's third wife. She had a sour disposition, but she was a mighty good cook.

The day was cold with occasional snowflakes drifting down from gray skies. The weather suited Levi's mood.

The company was good, as was the plentiful food. His grandfather's stories of holidays past had everyone chuckling. When the meal was over, Reuben stepped outside to smoke his pipe. Levi joined him. Few Amish smoked, but the occasional use of a pipe by an elder was permitted.

His grandfather's snow-white hair held a permanent crimp around his head from the hat he normally wore. His beard, as white as his hair, reached the center of the dark gray vest he had buttoned over his white shirt. His sharp eyes looked Levi up and down. "You are better?"

"I am."

"*Gotte es goot.* I heard those rascally brothers of yours played a pretty good prank on Daniel Hershberger and his new wife."

"I knew the story would get around quick. The twins rigged the seat to tip over backwards when the carriage started moving."

"So it is true? Daniel and Susan went rolling down the street with their feet in the air?"

Levi suppressed a grin. "Kicking like a pair of mad babies."

Reuben pulled his pipe from between his teeth and laughed out loud. "I wish I might have seen it."

"It was right funny, but what they did was no laughing matter. Had Daniel's horse run out into traffic, someone could have gotten hurt, or worse."

"True enough. What have you done about it?"

"I told the boys they had to find work elsewhere,"

"Did you?" Reuben looked surprised. He took a drag on his pipe and blew a ring of smoke in the air.

"Was I wrong?"

"That's not for me to say, Levi. You've dedicated your life to raising those boys. Many admire you for it, some call you foolish. A man rarely has the luxury of knowing if his decision was right or wrong in this life. How did they take it?"

"Better than I hoped."

"Have you thought about separating them?"

"What do you mean?"

"I'm thinking it might be good for them to get along without each other for a time. Your cousin Mark from over in Berlin could put one of the boys to work on his dairy farm. Leah Belier told Lydia her cousin was looking for help in his construction business in Sugarcreek. He and his family are staying with her until tomorrow if you want to talk to him about it."

"The twins have never been away from each other."

"Unless they plan to remain old boys all their lives, that will have to change eventually."

"I will think on it." He would ask Sarah for her opinion. She had a knack for handling the boys.

A shriek came from inside the house. They hurried in to find Lydia beating the floor with a broom. The twins were doubled over with laughter.

Atlee said, "It's just a plastic spider."

"The look on your face was priceless." Moses caught sight of Levi's stern face and smothered his grin.

"Oh, you evil boys. I hate spiders, and you know it." Lydia left the room with a huff.

"You're lucky my wife didn't take that broom to your backsides." Reuben sent a speaking glance at Levi.

He knew what his grandfather meant. It was time the boys learned to go their separate ways. He would speak to his cousin Mark and to Leah's cousin.

He nodded. "I reckon you are right. It's time we should be leaving. Gideon and Rebecca, it was a mighty good meal. Merry Christmas to you all. Grandfather, please tell Lydia I'm sorry for her fright. The boys will be over this week to cut and stack a cord of wood for her."

The expressions on the boys' faces changed from

amusement to outrage. Levi fixed his gaze on them and added sternly, "And they will be happy to do it."

Reuben grinned and patted the boys on their shoulders. "You will find many changes in store for you in the next few weeks. If I were you boys, I'd be on my best behavior."

Moses glanced from his grandfather to Levi. "What is that supposed to mean?"

Levi said, "We'll talk about it after supper tonight. It's time to go."

To his surprise, the twins didn't pester him for an explanation on the way home. When they arrived at the house, he waited until the boys got out, then he said, "I've got to see someone. I'll be home in a couple of hours."

"Where are you going?" Atlee asked.

"To Leah Belier's place."

The twins exchanged hard glances with each other. Levi snapped the lines against his horse's rump and drove away. It was four miles to Leah's home. He would have plenty of time to wonder if he was doing the right thing before he reached her house. He half hoped her cousin would be gone by the time he arrived.

Sarah had been waiting for Levi to come home. When she saw them pull up, she hurried to put on her coat, gathered her gift and headed out the front door. But by the time she reached her front gate, Levi was turning the corner at the end of the street. The twins were standing in their front yard watching him leave.

Disappointed, she decided her gift might as well be given to the twins. She walked toward them with a large package wrapped in white butcher's paper in her arms and said, "Good evening to you both. I have a little something I thought you might like."

Atlee looked at her brightly. "What is it?"

"It's a smoked ham. I thought you might enjoy it for supper or keep it for Christmas dinner."

Amos Fisher had stopped by with it earlier. She didn't think he would mind if the Beachy family enjoyed some of his generosity. It would take her ages to finish so much meat.

"Where is Levi going?" She hadn't intended to show such interest, but she couldn't help herself.

"He's going to see his girlfriend," Moses grumbled.

"We don't know that Leah is his girlfriend," Atlee said, quickly.

Moses rolled his eyes. "I'm pretty sure he's not taking reading and writing lessons. Thanks for the ham, Sarah."

*"Du bischt wilkumm,"* she replied, handing it to him.

They were welcome to the ham even though she had hoped to make Levi smile when she told him where it came from. Amos Fisher had only one hundred and ninety-nine sows left now. Tonight, Levi wouldn't be smiling at her joke. He'd be smiling at something Leah said or making her laugh.

Sarah sighed and looked at Moses. "Are you going to the winter picnic at Leah's place on Saturday?"

"Are you?" Atlee asked.

"I'm not sure. My brother and his family are coming to visit. It depends on when they leave. What about you?"

Moses scowled. "That's a party for old folks. We don't want the gang thinking we're part of the goody-goody crowd. We're going to the hoedown at Ezra Bowman's farm."

"I heard Sally Yoder mention it. Ben Lapp seemed to think it might be a wild party."

"That's the best kind," Atlee said with a grin.

"You boys will be careful, won't you? I've heard that some of the kids in that gang drink and do drugs."

"We'll be careful. We don't need to drink to have a good time," Moses assured her with a twinkle in his eyes.

"That's very sensible."

"We don't need to, but it helps!" Atlee yelled.

The boys dashed up the steps and into the house before she could say anything else.

She curbed her need to scold them and held tight to the knowledge that most Amish boys gave up their wild teenage ways and became good husbands and fathers. She would pray that Levi's brothers soon discovered worldly pleasures weren't as satisfying as leading a quiet, plain life with their loved ones and friends close at hand. It would break Levi's heart if they strayed from the Amish way of life and were lost to the wickedness of the world.

Sarah looked up to heaven. "Lord, what those boys need is a sign from You to make them see the error of their ways."

When she thought of all Levi had done for them and how little they seemed to care, she frowned. "I dearly wish I could see You deliver it."

## Chapter Thirteen

Levi got his wish. Leah's cousin had already gone by the time he reached her home. She gave Levi her brother's address in Sugarcreek and encouraged him to write and ask about a position for one of the boys. Like Levi's grandfather, she thought spending some time apart would be good for them.

Over the next several days, Levi saw little of Sarah. Her family had arrived and she was kept busy with her houseful. On the Monday before Christmas, he had a chance to become reacquainted with her brother when he came by the shop.

Vernon was several years older than Levi, but he remembered him from school. "You're the boy my sister shoved in the creek, aren't you? I heard about that from the girls."

The reminder wasn't as painful as it once had been. "I reckon I deserved it."

"It was Bethany's doing. She thought it was a pretty good joke, but I don't think she ever told Sarah. Poor Sarah, she felt so bad. She always thought she was the reason you left school before graduation."

"My dad needed me in the shop."

"I thought that must be it. That last year of school was a waste for me. I wanted to be out and working. I thought I'd be working in the mill alongside my father. Instead, I married a woman with a dairy farm. Luckily, we have her nephews who help us or we wouldn't be able to come for this visit. Cows never take a day off."

Levi smiled at the boy hanging on Vernon's leg. "What's your name?"

"Merle."

"Nice to meet you. How old are you, Merle?"

"Five. I'm gonna go to school next year." He was dressed exactly like his father, with dark pants, a dark coat and a wide-brimmed black hat.

"Are you enjoying your visit with your aunt Sarah?" Levi asked.

"She's gonna take me fishing today," the tyke announced proudly.

Leaning down, Levi propped his hands on his knees and said, "I'd stand clear when she tries to cast if I were you. She's not very good at it."

"I heard that," Sarah said from the doorway.

He saw her approaching with a woman he assumed was her sister-in-law and two little girls.

Vernon introduced his wife, Alma, and his daughters Rosanna and Phoebe. Rosanna, who looked to be about eleven or twelve, stood quietly by her mother's side. She reminded him of Sarah at that age. Phoebe was a few years younger. She hung back behind her mother's skirts and clutched a blank-faced doll.

Alma said, "I can't wait to do some of my Christmas shopping. What a treat it is to stay in town. Vernon, are you sure you'll be okay with the *kinder* while I'm gone?"

"Don't worry about us. Come, children, let us hitch up your aunt Sarah's buggy for Mother so she doesn't have to walk the streets with her arms full of packages." He herded the kids out the door.

Alma said, "Sarah, I forgot my shawl in the house. I'll be right back."

Levi found himself alone with Sarah. The ease with which he'd once spoken to her deserted him. He wanted nothing more than to take her in his arms and hold her close. He needed to know how she felt about him. He needed to know if there was any hope for him. Could she love him even a little?

The questions he wanted to ask stuck in his throat. Fear made him keep silent.

When her family left the shop, Sarah crossed her arms and smiled after them. "I can't believe how much those children have grown since I last saw them. Rosanna has put off her *eahmal shatzli.*"

The *eahmal shatzli* or "long apron" was the traditional dress of young Amish girls. When a girl was allowed to "put it off" and wear the short apron and cape like her mother, it was a sign that she was moving into womanhood.

Levi said, "She looks like you did at her age."

"She's much prettier than I was and so bright. She reminds me of Bethany."

"Sarah, I need to speak to you," he blurted out in a rush.

From outside, Alma called, "Sarah, I'm ready."

The door opened and young Walter Knepp came in. The teenager looked around and asked, "Where are the twins?"

Sarah took a step closer to Levi. "You look so serious, Levi. What's the matter?"

He couldn't do it. Not with people watching and waiting on them. He needed to find a time when they wouldn't be interrupted.

"Never mind. It can wait. Enjoy your shopping trip.

Walter, the twins are at the harness shop chopping wood for their grandfather."

Walter left but Sarah remained. "Are you sure it can wait?"

He nodded. "I'm sure."

"Okay."

She started to leave but paused at the door. "We're going to eat at the café tomorrow evening. Would you like to join us? The twins are welcome, as well."

He felt as if a weight had fallen off his back. "I'd like that."

Her eyes sparkled with delight. "Wonderful."

Sarah had been right about one thing. Having children in the house kept her from dwelling on the sadness of holidays past.

Rosanna was a quiet child, but Merle never walked if he could run and he ran as often as possible. Her fishing trip with him to Elam Sutter's pond was half a success. She had a nice visit with Katie Sutter, and Merle caught four fish but none that were big enough to keep, much to his disappointment.

The following evening, Levi was waiting beside her gate when they came outside. Sarah looked around. "Where are the twins?"

"I decided not to risk spoiling your brother's visit by subjecting his family to them."

"So you didn't invite them?"

"Nope. I decided not to spoil my evening by subjecting myself to them."

"They aren't that bad, Levi."

"That's what you think."

As her family piled in her buggy, Sarah found herself wedged between Levi and the children in the backseat while her brother drove through the quiet streets of town. Along the way, they enjoyed the Christmas lights and display in the English homes and businesses.

"Oh, how beautiful," Rosanna said when they passed the stately pine in the center of the town square. It was covered with multicolored lights and bore a shining silver star on the highest branch.

Phoebe turned to her father. "Why can't we have a tree like that at our home? We have big pines."

Vernon shared a knowing glance with his wife and then said, "Sarah, do you remember asking Father that question? Why don't you tell Phoebe what her grandfather had to say about the subject?"

Sarah smiled softly at the warm childhood memory. "We were traveling to visit Aunt Emma, and we passed by this very tree. It was smaller then and so was I. I said, 'Papa, why can't we have pretty trees like the *Englisch?*'"

"What did he say?" Merle asked.

"He said that when our Lord and Savior was born, no one decorated a tree for him. No one put fancy lights on the roof of the lowly stable. Jesus came to us quietly, in a plain and simple way. We have no need of glowing lights to remind us of His coming, for His light is bright and strong in each of our hearts. And when Jesus looks down from heaven to see how we are celebrating his birth, He looks for the simple light that shines from inside us, where it counts. All those of us who keep His light in our hearts make a more beautiful display to His eyes than any English tree."

Vernon looked at his daughter. "So, Rosanna. Do you want God to see lights in our pine trees or do you want him to see the light in your heart."

"I want Him to see the light in my heart," Rosanna answered quietly.

"Me, too," Phoebe said.

"Me, three," Merle chimed in.

"Me, four," Sarah added. Levi took her hand and gave it a squeeze. She had let the light of God's love grow dim in her heart. The sorrows of the past could not be forgotten, but they could be endured.

Sarah couldn't remember when she'd had a more enjoyable evening. The food was excellent and made better by the fact that she didn't have to cook or clean up afterwards. She had pork roast so tender it fell apart when she put her fork in it. The green beans were steamed to perfection and the sweet potato fries were delicious. She didn't have room for dessert when she finished her meal. Levi had no trouble putting away a slice of peach pie topped with vanilla ice cream.

As they were getting ready to leave, Elam and Katie Sutter came in with their family. Seeing Levi, Elam stopped by the table with his infant son in his arms. The chubby baby sported a pearly white bottom tooth when he grinned at Merle and Phoebe's baby talk.

Levi looked to Elam. "Are you getting more sleep these days?"

"Finally."

The men grinned at each other and Elam left to join his wife and children in a booth at the back of the room.

Sarah's heart warmed as she imagined Levi with a child of his own. He'd learned some hard lessons raising his brothers and sister. Sarah suspected he would do things differently with his own son or daughter, for the better.

Vernon covered his mouth and coughed deeply, then he grimaced and rubbed his chest.

Alma looked at him with concern. "Are you sick?"

"I've got a scratchy throat, that's all."

Levi said, "Take care of yourself. There's a nasty flu bug making the rounds. I had it myself, and it wasn't fun."

He glanced at Sarah, but she couldn't tell what he was thinking. She looked away, afraid he would see how much that time alone with him had meant to her.

On the way back to the house, Sarah wished she lived miles from the inn instead of a dozen blocks. If she did, she'd be able to sit snuggled beside Levi for hours. As it was, they reached their destination all too quickly. Watching him walk home, she began to miss him before he was even out of sight.

Whenever Levi was near, she only wanted to keep him near. When he was away from her, all she wanted to do was to see him again.

The intensity of her feelings frightened her. How long could she keep them hidden if he loved another? How could she keep them from growing stronger?

Later, when she was ready for bed, Sarah knelt beside her mattress and prayed. She prayed that her feeling wouldn't grow into love.

She slept poorly, but it was the only rest she would get for many hours. Before dawn, there was a knock on Sarah's door and her sister-in-law came in.

Sarah sat up in bed. "What's wrong?"

"It's Vernon. He's very ill. Can you come help me?"

"It sure seems quiet over at Sarah's place. Has her family gone home?" Atlee stood at the workbench looking out the window.

Levi stopped working. "Their buggy was still parked beside Sarah's barn when I fed our horses this morning."

Atlee said, "Merle is normally up and about this time of the day. Usually, he's running back and forth along the fence hitting the pickets with a stick. It beats me why he gets such a thrill out of it."

Levi rose from his stool at the counter and moved to

the window. Movement at Sarah's kitchen window caught his eye. It looked as if Sarah's sister-in-law was crying and Sarah was comforting her. He said, "I think I'll go over and see if everything is all right."

He left the shop and hurried across the street. Sarah's front gate squeaked when he opened it. He would have to tell Atlee or Moses to oil it. Sarah opened the door before he reached it. Merle stood at her side.

"Is everything all right?" Levi asked.

"Papa is sick and we have to be quiet," Merle told him solemnly.

Sarah said, "I think it's the same flu that you had. So far, none of the rest of us are sick. What did you need?"

"Nothing. Atlee noticed Merle wasn't out banging on the picket fence. I wondered if everything was okay."

"Mamm says I can't make noise so *Daed* can sleep." Merle looked sorely disappointed.

"What can I do to help?" Levi asked.

She smiled, but she couldn't hide the fear in her eyes. "I am low on some medicines. Could you go to the drugstore for me?"

"Of course." He came inside while Sarah wrote up a list of things she needed. He wanted to hold her close and offer his comfort, but he didn't dare. He didn't know if she would welcome his attention. If only he had spoken before. As soon as he was granted another chance, he would accept it gladly. He couldn't bear not knowing how she felt.

After fetching her supplies, he returned as quickly as he could. He handed them over. "Would you like me to sit with Vernon for a while? You look tired."

"I didn't sleep well. I'm not worried about me. I'm worried about Alma. She's four months' pregnant, and it hasn't been an easy pregnancy for her. This stress isn't good for her or the babe. If we can't get Vernon's fever down in a few hours, I will send for the doctor."

"I'll be close by if you need me."

Her grim expression lightened. "I never doubted it for a minute. Can I ask you one more favor?"

"Anything."

"Can you take Merle with you for a few hours? He's restless."

"Sure. Atlee and Moses can take him to the park. I imagine he'd like the slide and the swings. They can take the girls, too. It's a cold day, but if they dressed warm, they should be okay."

"That's a great idea. I'll make sure it's okay with Alma, and I'll send them over when they're ready. Thanks for stopping by, Levi. You're a good friend."

He reached out and grasped her hand. "We're more than friends, Sarah. I hope you know that."

Panic flashed in her eyes, but she quickly subdued it. "Best friends," she said and withdrew her hand.

He had to leave it at that.

An hour later, Phoebe and Merle arrived at the shop. Levi looked out the door. "Where is Rosanna?"

Phoebe said, "She wanted to stay home even though *Mamm* says she can't be in Papa's room because she might get sick, too."

Atlee and Moses came forward when Levi beckoned to them. Moses said, "I can't believe we have to babysit. What if somebody from the gang sees us?"

Levi frowned at him. "You'll live. Do not forget all Sarah has done for us. This is the least we can do to ease her burdens."

Although the twins grumbled about being stuck with a pair of babies, they left the shop with the children happily tagging along behind them.

Levi waited, but Sarah didn't come get him that morning. He figured Vernon must be better. Sarah wouldn't hesitate to involve the doctor.

The twins returned with two tired children just before noon. When questioned, Levi discovered his brothers actually enjoyed spending time with the little ones. Merle was so taken with Moses that he asked if Moses would take him to the park again tomorrow.

Moses ruffled the boy's hair. "Sure, kid. Why not?"

Late Friday morning, Levi stopped in to check on Sarah again. She looked worn to the bone and more worried than ever. She offered him a seat at the kitchen table and a cup of coffee.

He asked, "Is Vernon worse?"

"No, but Alma has made herself sick with worry and work. I went to the Wilsons' down the street and used their phone to call the doctor. He's with Alma now."

"Is it the babe?"

Sarah nodded. "I can't bear to think of her losing her baby. Why can't we have one Christmas with something joyous to remember?"

The sound of the doctor's footsteps coming down the stairs had Sarah out of her seat. Her hands were clenched tightly together.

Dr. White came in the kitchen. A tall, dignified man with silver hair, the elderly physician was well past eighty, but still practiced in the community that he loved with the help of a partner. "I won't beat around the bush. She needs rest. She needs to stay in bed for a week at least. I'm going to send my granddaughter-in-law, Amber, over to give you a break, Sarah."

"*Danki,* Dr. White."

"Don't mention it. Alma is worried about her other children. Is there someone in the family who can keep them for a while? I think it would ease her mind and help her rest."

"I'm sure my Aunt Emma will be happy to take the children for a few days."

"Good. Call me if anything changes, Sarah."

Levi walked him outside. The doctor asked, "How are you? No lingering ill effects from your bout with this mean virus?"

"I feel fine."

"That's great. I hear there is a winter picnic out at Leah Belier's home tomorrow. I remember what fun they could be."

"You're welcome to come."

"No, these bones are too old to sit on hay bales around a bonfire. You young people go and enjoy yourselves while you can. See if you can get Sarah to go. She needs a break. She doesn't say anything, but I can tell she's under a lot of strain. It can't be easy having her only remaining sibling ill and lying in the same room where her husband died. For some reason, she thinks she is to blame because she invited them."

"I thought Vernon was getting better."

"Oh, he is, but I'm not sure Sarah can see that past the painful association she has with past events. It isn't rational, but for her it is a very real fear."

Levi shook his head. "I doubt she'll go to a picnic. I plan to stay home, as well. Someone should be close by if she needs help."

"You're probably right. I'll stop in at the Wadler Inn and ask Naomi Wadler to put the word out that Sarah could use an extra pair of hands."

The doctor settled his gray fedora on his head and glanced at the gray overcast sky. "My old bones think it's going to snow. They're usually right." He nodded to Levi and walked briskly up the street toward his clinic.

Levi was preoccupied with thoughts of Sarah as he entered the shop. The twins were working on a banged-up courting buggy that had ended up in a ditch when the driver should have been paying attention to the road and not the girl beside him.

Levi looked at the clock. It was getting late.

He spoke to the boys. "I've got to get going. Leah Belier is expecting me. If Sarah needs anything, I know she can count on you until I return."

Moses tipped his head to the side. "You've been seeing a lot of Leah lately. Is there something you want to tell us?"

"Not right now. Maybe later." He didn't want to say anything until he heard back from Leah's cousin about a job for only one of them in Sugarcreek.

"What does that mean?" Atlee asked.

"It means I may have news to tell you later but I don't have anything to say about it now."

Moses tipped his head toward the door. "Come on, Atlee, let's get the buggy ready for Levi while he gets cleaned up, or he'll be late for his date."

"And she may not wait." Atlee chuckled at his rhyme, but Levi just shook his head.

Moses said, "Leah hates it when people are late."

When Levi came out of the house a half hour later, his horse and buggy were waiting outside the front door. The twins were nowhere in sight. He caught sight of Sarah back by her barn slipping a headstall on her gray. Where was she headed?

He walked toward her. As much as he wanted to take her in his arms, he knew his timing couldn't have been worse. She had too much on her plate at the moment. She didn't need to hear his lovesick utterings. If only he could manage some time alone with her, then he might find the courage to tell her how he felt.

"Sarah, can I give you a lift somewhere? My horse is ready to go."

She turned around with a grateful sigh. "I need to take the children out to my Aunt Emma's farm. Naomi Wadler and Amber are sitting with Alma and Vernon so I thought I would go now and be back before dark."

Her aunt's farm wasn't exactly on the way to Leah's place, but he didn't mind the detour. Not if it meant spending time with Sarah. "I'll drive you out."

"Really? But where were you going?"

"To help Leah set up for the winter picnic. I honestly don't mind going a little out of my way."

"That's hardly a little out of your way." She bit her lip.

"Okay, I don't mind going a lot out of my way. I'll drop you off and pick you up in a few hours. You can fill Emma in on what's been happening and not have to rush off." Would she accept? It might give him the opportunity he'd been hoping for. Time alone with her.

"All right. I'm so tired, I was worried I'd fall asleep and who knows where old Gray would take us. I'll go get the children."

Levi could barely contain his excitement. Without the children in the buggy, he and Sarah would be alone on the ride home. He'd have a chance to tell her how his love for her had grown and discover if she could return those feelings.

His hands were ice-cold when they finally got under-way. He wanted to blame it on the rapidly deteriorating weather, but the truth was he was as nervous as a man could be. Merle was excited about the trip. Rosanna put up a weak protest. She didn't want to leave her mother.

Phoebe was quiet and held tightly to her doll. Sarah kept up a running conversation in an effort to reassure the children.

He put his horse into a fast trot. The sooner he delivered Sarah and the children to her aunt, the sooner he could finish his work at Leah's and be back in this same buggy for a leisurely ride home with Sarah at his side.

The snow quickly changed over to sleet, and then back to snow as they traveled. The road became slippery, even for his surefooted mare. A half hour later, they were rounding a curve on a steep hillside when Levi felt something shift in the buggy beneath him.

The horse felt it, too, and cocked her head to the side. Her move carried the vehicle to the shoulder of the road. Sarah grasped his arm just as the buggy lurched sharply.

In horrifying slow motion, the buggy tipped over and tumbled down the ravine. He heard Sarah scream his name and then everything went black.

## Chapter Fourteen

Levi pressed a hand to his aching head. He winced when he felt the lump above his right eye. The sound of whimpering slowly registered in his foggy brain. He tried to sit up, but someone lay sprawled across his chest. Forcing his eyes to focus, he realized it was Rosanna.

He moved her gently to the side. "Rosanna, are you hurt?"

"Yes."

"Where, honey?"

"My face hurts."

He sat up and looked. She had a knot forming on her cheekbone that would turn into a bad bruise and a nasty gash on her chin. The good news was that it had stopped bleeding. He searched for the other children. Where were they? Where was Sarah?

The buggy lay smashed against a tree at the bottom of a steep hillside. Snow was quickly covering the splintered wood. A large black shape moved off to one side. He realized it was his mare. She was on her knees and struggling in the tangled harness.

"Sarah!" he shouted into the night.

"Levi?" came a weak reply. It was Merle.

Levi crawled toward the sound. He found the boy sitting on what once had been a door. "Merle, are you okay?"

"I'm scared."

"I'm scared, too. Where is Phoebe? Where is Sarah?"

"I don't know. What's wrong with your horse?"

"I'll see to her in a minute. I have to find the others. Sarah!" he shouted as loud as he could.

"She's with me." The voice belonged to Phoebe and it came from up the hillside.

Levi took the boy in his arms and carried him back to Rosanna. "Stay here."

He quickly worked his way up the steep slope where he found Phoebe sitting beside Sarah who lay sprawled sideways across the hill.

To his relief, she was breathing.

*Thank You, dear Lord, for sparing her.*

He looked at Phoebe. "Are you injured, child?"

"My hand hurts real bad."

"Let me see." She held it out. She had two dislocated fingers. His stomach took a wild flop, but he knew what he had to do. He searched around and found her doll nearby.

"Phoebe, I want you to bite down on your dolly's legs as hard as you can. Will you do that for me?"

"I don't want to bite her."

"This is important. She's going to help make your hand better, but you have to close your eyes and bite hard. She won't mind. She wants to help."

"Do as he says, Phoebe." Rosanna called from below.

Phoebe bit down on her doll and he quickly jerked her fingers back into place. She screamed and then fell back.

Rosanna struggled up the hill toward her.

Levi said, "She's okay. She just fainted."

He turned his attention to Sarah and lifted her gently in his lap. "Sarah, speak to me," he begged.

Her *kapp* was missing, and there was blood covering the side of her face. After a moment, her eyes fluttered open. Relief made him giddy.

*Thank You, God. I will never again miss the chance to tell this woman how much I love her.*

Sarah gazed up at him. Slowly, she raised her hand and touched his face. "You're alive."

"We all are."

"The children?" She tried to sit up, but he wasn't willing to let her go.

He glanced over his shoulder. Phoebe was sitting, supported between Merle and Rosanna. "They're banged up, but nothing too bad as far as I can see. What about you? Tell me where it hurts."

"I'm not sure." She touched her head and winced. Squinting, she moved her hand in front of her face and stared at her fingers. "Is that blood?"

Pellets of sleet mixed in with the snow stung Levi's face. He needed to get her and the children to shelter. "Do you think you can stand? We need to get out of this weather."

"I'll try."

He lifted her to her feet but she crumpled against him with a cry of pain. "My knee. It won't hold me."

He lowered her to the ground. "Which one?"

"The right one. This is all my fault. I shouldn't have invited them to visit. I knew something bad would happen."

"Sarah, you didn't cause this."

"You don't understand. Everyone I love is in danger."

She must have hit her head harder than he thought. She wasn't making sense. He sought to soothe her. "Don't fret. The children are going to be fine."

With gentle fingers, he examined her leg. Her knee was already swelling. "I can't tell if it is sprained or worse."

She looked at her nieces and nephew huddled together.

"If you can help me to the buggy, Levi, I'll wait here while you take the *kinder* to safety."

"I'm not leaving you."

"I'll be fine. Just take care of the children. Please, Levi."

"This is going to hurt." He slipped his arm beneath her knees and lifted her. She clutched his shoulders and bit her lip but didn't cry out. He carried her to the wreckage of the buggy. It was useless as a shelter. He lowered her to the snow-covered ground. There was no way he was going to leave her here alone. He looked at the children. They would all have to go together.

Leaving them briefly, he moved to his horse. She had stopped struggling and lay quietly on the ground. "Easy, my girl. I'll get you loose." He managed to unbuckle and lift the harness from her. She surged to her feet, but limped heavily as she managed a few steps. She wouldn't be able to carry Sarah or the children.

He searched for a suitable place to leave her and found it beneath a leaning cedar. Leading her slowly, he tied her under the makeshift canopy knowing she would be safe until he could return for her.

Moving back to Sarah and the children, he surveyed what they had and what they would need. The first thing was to get up the hill to the roadway and hope they could flag down a passing vehicle. It was unlikely this time of day and in this weather. Barring that, they would simply have to walk to the home of Sarah's aunt.

He said, "Rosanna, I need you to unbuckle one of the long lines from my horse's bridle."

To his relief, she quickly did as he asked. When she came back with the leather strap he said, "Now, I want you to make three loops for handholds about three feet apart."

"Like this?" she asked as she tied the first one.

*"Ja."*

"I'm cold," Phoebe whined.

Merle said, "I want Mama."

Sarah said, gently, "Darling, Levi is going to take you to *Aenti* Emma's. I want you to do as he tells you."

Rosanna held up the rein with three loops in it. "Is this right?"

He took it from her. "Couldn't have done better myself."

He tied one end around his waist, and then squatted so he was eye level with the children. "I want each one of you to put your hand through a loop. Rosanna, I want you on the end so that the little ones are between us. If everyone holds on, no one can get lost. Okay?"

The children nodded. He looked at Phoebe. "I need your apron to make a bandage for your sore hand. Is that okay?" She nodded. He fashioned a makeshift sling and some padding for her arm. It was the best he could do.

Rosanna quickly fastened the loops around her sister's good hand and then placed one over Merle's.

Levi moved to pick up Sarah. She tried to push him away. "You can't carry me all the way to my uncle's farm. I will only slow you down."

"Sarah, the longer you keep talking, the longer these children have to stand here in the cold." He scooped her up in his arms and ignored her hiss of pain. It couldn't be helped.

He stared up the hillside. It would be a steep climb at the best of times. At night, in the snow, with Sarah in his arms, it was going to be a nightmare.

He looked at the children lined up behind him. "Ready?"

They all nodded. Levi began making his way up the slope with careful steps. The wet snow made the climbing treacherous. It wasn't any easier for the children behind him. Each time one of them slipped and fell, he felt the jerk on the line at his waist. He struggled to keep his feet.

His arms ached with the strain, but he didn't stop. By the time they reached the top and the roadway, everyone was out of breath and panting. Merle began crying.

"The hard part is over, dearest," Sarah said with her face buried in Levi's neck. Her voice had grown weaker.

The steep part was over. Levi wasn't sure they were past the hard part. "This way," he said, and started walking.

They had only gone a little ways when Rosanna called out, "Can we rest now?"

"Sure." Levi dropped to one knee, allowing Sarah's weight to rest on his leg and give his aching arms a much-needed break. She still had her face buried against his neck. If the children weren't present, he would have kissed her and professed his love again and again.

That would have to wait until they were all safe, but the sun would not set tomorrow before he found a way to be alone with Sarah and make his feelings known. Did she care for him at all? He prayed that she could find it in her heart to love him a little.

He struggled to his feet. "Time to go."

Merle refused to get up. "I can't go on. I'm tired. I want my *daed* to come get me."

"Great," Levi muttered as he sank to his knee again. He couldn't carry Sarah and drag the children, too.

"They are scared, Levi. Talk to them. Take their minds off what they have to do." Sarah's voice was weaker. He worried about the blow to her head. How serious was it?

He said, "Merle, I heard you're quite a fisherman. Is that true?"

*"Ja,"* came the small reply.

Levi rose to his feet and hefted Sarah to a more comfortable position. "What's the biggest fish you've caught?"

"I caught a four-pound bass at our pond." Merle's voice grew stronger. "It was a whopper."

Levi cocked his head to the side and said in mock disbelief, "Four pounds? *Nee, not* a little fella like you."

Merle rose to his feet. "I'm stronger than I look."

Levi hid a grin. "I believe you. Girls, what about you?" He started walking. The children moved close to his side.

Rosanna said, "I caught a six-pound blue cat down at the river."

"Are you sure it was a blue catfish and not a channel cat? Merle, did you see it?"

"It was a blue cat all right."

"Some channel cats can look blue." Levi kept a slow pace, even though his mind screamed at him to hurry for Sarah's sake.

Merle said, "Channel cats have spots on their sides."

Levi asked, "Did it have spots, Rosanna?"

"Not a one."

Phoebe said, "I caught a pumpkin seed."

"You did?" Levi pretended to be impressed.

Merle looked up at Levi. "It wasn't very big."

"But it was real pretty," Phoebe insisted.

Levi said, "I reckon it was. I think pumpkin seeds are about the prettiest fish around. What about you, Rosanna?"

"I saw a goldfish in a store once. It was beautiful. It had a long tail that looked like a ribbon."

"You don't say?"

"I saw it, too." Merle jumped in to support her claim.

Phoebe said, "I'm cold. Can we stop now?"

"Not yet, Phoebe. We still have a little ways to go."

"How far?" she demanded.

"Look up ahead. I see a light in the window. Do you see it?"

Phoebe said, "I don't see anything."

"I do," Levi insisted. It was an exaggeration on his part. He couldn't see more than twenty yards through the snow, but he knew a light was shining in the darkness, waiting to guide them to safety.

"Is it a Christmas candle?" Rosanna asked.

He smiled down at her. "That's right. It's a Christmas candle in your aunt's window. It's meant to remind all of us that Christ is the light of the world."

Merle said, "Christmas is God's birthday."

"It's His son's birthday. We did a play about the birth of Jesus for our school program," Rosanna told them.

Levi's aching arms couldn't hold Sarah any longer. He said, "Let's rest a moment."

He dropped to one knee again. *Please, Lord, give me the strength I need.*

"I'm so sorry this happened. I can stay here while you go on." Sarah's voice was weak, her words slurred together.

He redoubled his resolve and struggled to his feet. "I was just giving the kids a break. Rosanna, tell us about your play while we walk."

Phoebe said, "I was one of the angels."

Sarah's arm slipped from around his neck. "Stay with me, Sarah. Did you hear? Phoebe was an angel in her school play."

"I know." Relief flooded him at the sound of Sarah's voice.

"Who did you play, Rosanna?" she asked.

"I played the innkeeper's wife."

Merle said, "I'd be Joseph if I was old enough to go to school."

"You will be old enough one day, Merle." Levi squinted to see ahead of them. Was it his imagination? No, there was a light.

"Are we there yet?" Phoebe asked.

"We are. This is the lane and up ahead is your Aunt Emma's house. Can you see it?"

"I see it." Rosanna's voice brimmed with relief.

"Me, too." Merle dropped his loop and ran ahead.

When Levi and the girls arrived, Emma and her husband were at the door. Emma quickly stripped the wet coats from the children and wrapped them in quilts while her husband helped Levi carry Sarah to the sofa.

When she was safely surround by her family, Levi said, "She needs a doctor. She hit her head pretty hard. May I use your buggy?"

Abe patted Levi's shoulder. "You get out of that wet coat and warm up, son. I'll fetch the doctor."

Levi gave his coat to Emma and sank into Abe's chair.

"Levi?" Sarah called his name and raised her hand. He was on his knees beside her in an instant.

He took her cold hand in his. "What, Sarah?"

"I've never heard you talk so much in all the years I've known you. You were wonderful. You saved us all."

"Rest, Sarah. I'll be right here if you need me."

"I never doubted it for a moment." She closed her eyes and drifted off to sleep. Levi closed his eyes, too, and gave thanks to God for sparing the life of the woman he loved.

Sunlight was streaming through the window when Sarah opened her eyes. The room in which she lay was vaguely familiar. A sharp headache pounded behind her eyes. Slowly, the events of the previous night came back to her and she realized she was in her aunt's home.

She tried to sit up but the effort was too much. It made her knee hurt insanely. She grimaced and lay back. Memories of their horrid mishap flashed through her mind. Levi and the children had come so close to death. Once again, the ones she loved had been made to suffer. She folded her hands and bowed her head.

*Thank You, Lord, for sparing Levi and the children.*

*Please, God, I won't love him if only you'll keep him safe.
I'll be happy for him and Leah, I promise. Have pity on
me. Don't make me endure another loss.*

"Are you awake, child?" her aunt asked from the door.
Sarah opened her eyes. "I am. How are the children?"

"Their cuts and scrapes have all been tended. They are
fine, but Merle seems to be particularly upset. He says he
won't go back inside a buggy."

"The poor child. And Levi? He was so sick only a week
ago." Only bad things had happened to him since her feelings for him had begun to change. She couldn't cause him
more pain. She wouldn't.

"Levi seems fine for a man who didn't get a wink of
sleep for worrying about you. He did put away a good
breakfast this morning. That's always a sign a man is feeling well. He wants to see you when you're awake. Shall I
send him in now?"

Could she face him without revealing her love? Somehow, she had to. "I will see him."

Her aunt went out. The door opened again and Levi
peeked in. "How are you?"

"Oh, look at your poor face. You have a black eye." It
was all her fault. If he had gone straight to Leah's home,
none of this would have happened. Why did everyone she
love end up getting hurt?

"I've had worse than this." He dismissed her concern.

He might pretend it didn't bother him, but Sarah knew
better. It must hurt as much as her knee. How had he found
the strength to carry her so far?

*Don't think about how much you want to be held in his
arms again.*

She stared at the quilt pattern on the bed. "What happened last night?"

"We lost a wheel and tipped over in the worst possible spot. But we are all alive to tell the tale. God was merciful."

God had shown mercy last night, but what about next time? She couldn't bear the thought of losing Levi. It would be painful to see him happy with Leah, but she could live with that if he was safe.

He moved closer and pulled a chair to the side of her bed. Her heart started beating like crazy.

He took her hand and gazed into her eyes. "I'm so thankful you are safe, Sarah. Last night, when I came to in the buggy and couldn't find you, I thought I would never have the chance to tell you this. I love you, Sarah."

Her eyes flew open wide. "No, you don't."

"I know my own heart. I do love you. What I don't know is how you feel."

*Terrified. Wonderful. Sad. If only I could love you in return, but I don't dare. My heart is breaking, but you can never know that.*

She looked out the window. "You're simply feeling guilty about the accident. You don't love me. You are in love with Leah."

"Leah? Why would you think that?"

She looked at him and saw astonishment written on his face. "I saw you kiss her."

He shook his head. "I don't know who you saw kissing Leah, but it surely wasn't me."

Had she been mistaken? No, she had seen Leah in his arms. "The day you sold her a new buggy, I saw you holding her in the shop. She was in your arms. You were about to kiss her. And that's fine. She is a wonderful woman."

"She had a cinder in her eye. I was trying to get it out. I wasn't going to kiss her. The thought never crossed my mind. It is you I wish to kiss, Sarah Wyse. If you can love me even half as much as you loved Jonas, I will spend my life trying to make you happy. Say that you will marry me."

Sarah froze. She couldn't draw a breath. Here was what she had longed for and what she feared. For a few wonderful seconds she thought that happiness could be hers again, but she forced that dream out of her heart. He'd almost been killed last night. As much as she wanted to return his love, she knew what she had to do.

She closed her eyes. She couldn't love him. If she did, he might be the next to die. Dying herself would be easier than losing him.

*Please, Lord. Don't do this to me. Levi needs a woman who will love him without doubt and without fear. I'm not brave enough.*

She turned her face away. "I don't love you, Levi."

The moment the words left her lips she knew they were a lie. She did love him. With all her heart.

Silence hung thick in the air. He let go of her hand. She heard his chair scrape back. What had she done?

At the sound of the door opening, she looked to him. "Levi?"

He paused without looking back.

"We can still be friends, can't we? Like it was before?" Oh, how she needed to have him near. It wasn't enough, but it was something.

He left the room without answering. When he closed the door, she burst into tears.

She was still sobbing when her aunt came in a short time later. Murmuring, "There, there." Emma gathered her close and held her until her tears finally ran dry.

Emma put a hand under Sarah's chin and lifted her face. "You refused him?"

Sarah sniffed. "How did you know? Did he say something?"

"Nothing needed to be said. I could tell from the way the light died in his eyes that you sent him away. I thought… I hoped that you had found love again, Sarah. I'm rarely mistaken about these things. Do you love him?"

She couldn't utter the lie a second time. "Yes."

"Then why send Levi away?"

"God has shown me His plan for me. He took Jonas from me. He took my sister and my parents. I must live alone. It is His will."

"Nonsense!" Her aunt scowled at her.

"What if I accepted Levi and he died, too? You don't understand." Sarah was too tired to explain herself.

Emma said, "I understand fear. I understand regret. I understand that it is hard to trust that God knows best. Yes, you have suffered great losses, Sarah. No one can deny that, but to think God wants you to spend your life without love is to say that He doesn't love you. Surely you believe in God's love."

"Of course I do."

"He loves you beyond all understanding."

"I know that."

"So you say, but do you truly believe it?"

Did she? Or did she doubt God's love? Was that why it was so hard to trust that He would bring love back into her life?

She shook her head. "I'm tired, *Aenti*. I'd like to try and sleep now."

She wanted to close her eyes and let the darkness swallow her. She didn't want to think, didn't want to feel.

"Very well." Emma rose from the side of the bed.

At the door, she turned back to Sarah. "If you don't believe God wishes you to be happy, why has Levi stayed beside you all these years? Think about that. Don't let fear rule your heart and ruin your life. Give it to God."

After her aunt was gone, Sarah turned gingerly to her side. Outside the window, the snow was still falling. She hated the snow.

Why had Levi stayed? Was that part of God's plan for them? If only she could believe it.

# *Chapter Fifteen*

Levi stepped down from Adrian Lapp's buggy. "Thanks for the lift."

"Not a problem. I'm happy to help. *Mamm* said they would bring the children back later this afternoon. Dr. White wants Sarah to rest her leg another day before trying to come home. He won't have any trouble keeping her and Alma in bed. There will be a half dozen women here to help take care of them by tomorrow night."

"That's good." The mere mention of Sarah's name sent a stab of pain though Levi's chest so sharp that he wanted to look and see if he was bleeding. She didn't love him. Not even a little.

He walked into his house and stopped in surprise. Grace stood at the kitchen sink peeling potatoes. She turned to smile at him and shrieked, "Levi! What happened to you?"

He heard his brothers pounding down the stairs. Moses said, "It must have been a hot date. You were gone all… night." He stopped dead in his tracks and his voice trailed away at the sight of Levi's face. Atlee bumped into him from behind.

Grace sped into action. "Sit down, Levi. Let me get some ice for you. Do you need to see a doctor?"

Could Dr. White reach inside him and put his shattered heart back together? If so, he'd go for treatment in a minute. "It's only a black eye, Grace. I didn't think you'd be home for another week."

"I learned what I needed to know so I came home. What happened to you?" she asked again as she gathered ice cubes from the freezer. The twins had come to stand on either side of him but they were surprisingly quiet.

"The left front wheel of the buggy came off when I was going around the hill out on Paint Road. The buggy swerved off the road, flipped over and rolled down the hill. I got off lucky. Sarah and the kids were banged up pretty good."

"Sarah and the kids were with you? Why? What were you doing on Paint Road?" Atlee demanded. His face had turned ashen.

Levi sat down and accepted the towel full of ice that Grace handed him. "I was going to drop them off at Emma Lapp's place so the children could stay there until their parents were well. The buggy is a complete loss."

Atlee went to look out the window. "What about Dotty? Where is she?"

"Jonathan Dresher came and got her with his horse ambulance. He's going to try to save her, but her front left leg is messed up pretty good. She'll never pull a buggy again."

"No!" Atlee grasped his hair with both hands.

Moses hadn't said a word. He sat down beside Levi. "How bad were the children hurt?"

"Rosanna's pretty face will have a jagged scar across her chin. She was badly bruised. Phoebe has bruises galore and two dislocated fingers on her hand." He shuddered when he thought about his crude fix for her.

"What about Merle?" Moses asked quietly.

Levi shook his head. "A few bumps and bruises on the

outside, but he started screaming bloody murder when we tried to put him inside a closed buggy. Finally, we gave up. Ben Lapp is bringing him home in his courting buggy. Merle won't get into anything else."

Moses folded his arms on the table and laid his head on them. "We did it. We rigged the wheel to come off."

Levi placed a hand on his brother's head. "I know. This morning, I went back for our horse. I found the axel nut on the roadway where the wheel dropped off. I saw at once it was the one for the wrong wheel."

Moses looked up with tears in his eyes. "I'm so sorry, Levi. I didn't mean to hurt anyone."

"Why did you do it?"

Atlee said, "We didn't want you to court Leah Belier. We thought if you stood her up for a date she might get mad and not go out with you anymore. The road to her place is long and flat. We thought the wheel would just drop off and you'd have to walk home."

An amazed bark of laughter broke from Levi. He shook his head. "That was a really stupid reason made all the more idiotic by the fact that I'm not courting Leah Belier."

"But you've been taking her for rides in your buggy. You've never taken a woman riding before."

"I was helping a friend. I'm not sure either of you would understand that."

He looked at Grace. "You are free to marry the man of your choice. Choose wisely, little sister."

He glanced at his brothers. "You boys have a decision to make. I'm moving to Colorado. I'll be leaving the day after Christmas."

"You don't mean that." Grace stared at him in shock.

"What about us?" the twins demanded.

Levi sighed. "You may come with me, or you may stay here. If you stay here and run the repair shop, you will have to negotiate a new contract with Sarah. She is well within her rights to refuse you."

"Was Sarah hurt?" Grace asked

"She injured her knee and can't walk. She also has a concussion." He rose to his feet.

Grace grabbed his hand. "I'm so thankful you were not badly injured for I dearly love you, brother. Please, don't leave Hope Springs."

He *was* badly injured, but not all wounds were as visible as his black eye. "My mind is made up. Atlee and Moses, I forgive you for the harm you have done me. I must go and pack. I don't need any help. I'd like to be alone for a while."

He walked up the stairs, leaving stunned silence behind him.

Sarah used the crutches the doctor had given her to make her way into her house. Her aunt and uncle had taken the children home the day before. Inside, Vernon was pacing the floor. The moment he saw her, he rushed to her, took her by the shoulders and kissed both her cheeks. "Praise God for His mercy."

"How is Alma?"

"She was a wreck, but once the children arrived, she went straight back to bed as the doctor had ordered. She is reading them a story now."

The front door opened and Grace Beachy walked in. Her eyes were puffy from crying. She threw her arms around Sarah. "I'm so sorry for the pain my family caused you."

"It's all right. I'm glad you are back." She was happy to see her friend. It meant she wouldn't have to work in the shop with Levi any more. Things could get back to normal.

Levi would soon realize he didn't love her. They could be friends again. Tears stung her eyes at the thought.

"Sarah, Levi is leaving Hope Springs. He's moving away," Grace said between sniffles.

Sarah's heart dropped to her feet. "What?"

"He told us he is leaving town for good. His bus leaves at four o'clock the day after Christmas. We've tried to talk him out of it, but he won't be swayed. What are we going to do without him?"

"Where is he? I can't let him do this."

"He's in the shop."

Her brother said, "Shouldn't you be lying down? The doctor said to rest that knee."

"I will. After I've spoken with Levi."

He couldn't leave. How would she repair the damage she had done to their friendship if he moved away? He had to stay. She couldn't bear it if he left.

She hobbled across the street on her crutches, pulled open the door and went in. He was standing in front of the workbench sorting his tools. He didn't glance up. "What do you want, Sarah?"

He must have seen her crossing the street.

"Grace tells me you're leaving." She still couldn't believe it.

"I am." He didn't look at her.

Why wouldn't he look at her?

Tears gathered in her eyes, but she blinked them back. "Are you really going to Colorado?"

He carefully wrapped his tools in a length of canvas. *"Ja."*

She didn't want him to go. She needed him. Her life would go back to being empty with nothing but work to fill the lonely hours if he were gone.

*You mean so much to me, Levi. Please turn around and look at me.*

He didn't. Suddenly, the truth sank in. She had lost

him. Her fear had robbed them both of a chance at happiness. A tear slipped down her cheek. "I hope you'll be happy there."

He threw down his tools and raised his face to heaven. There was such sorrow in his expression. "How can I be happy if I'm not near you?"

"Then why are you leaving?"

He turned to face her. The pain in his eyes cut her like a knife. "Not so very long ago, I told myself that I could be content if you loved me just a fraction of the way you loved Jonas. But I was fooling myself, Sarah. I'm a selfish man. If you cannot love me every bit as much or more than you loved Jonas, then I must go. I can't be satisfied watching you through the window anymore. I love you, but if you don't love me, leaving is all that is left."

"I care for you, Levi. You know that."

"But do you love me?"

How could she make him understand? "I want to."

He closed his eyes and turn away. She couldn't let him go. "I want to love you, but I'm afraid, Levi."

He turned back to her. "What is it you fear? Surely you know I would never hurt you."

"I'm afraid you'll die," she whispered the words, as if saying them aloud would give them power. She covered her face with her hands.

"What do you mean?"

"Everyone I love dies. You and the children were almost killed because of me." She tried to leave but stumbled on her crutches. He caught her and held her in his arms.

"Oh, Sarah." His voice softened. "The wreck wasn't your fault. My brothers rigged the wheel to come off."

She tried to turn her face away from him. "How it happened doesn't matter."

"You're right. I'm going to die. We are all going to die, Sarah. Not loving someone won't prevent that."

"It's all I can do. You have to be safe."

"You can't keep me safe any more than you can take the moon out of the sky. All you can do is make living bearable for me. Sarah, one day of knowing your love would make my entire life worthwhile, no matter how short or how long."

"Don't say that."

"Don't speak the truth? How can you ask me to lie? I love you, Sarah. How many times must I say it? God planted this love in my heart. He allowed it to grow into something strong and enduring. It will not die even after I'm laid in my grave. I will love you through eternity, as God is my witness, I will."

She broke down and sobbed.

Levi couldn't bear the sight of her tears any longer. He gathered her into his arms and held her tight. Her hands grasped his coat as if she were afraid to let go.

"Don't cry, *liebschen*. Please, don't cry so."

She pressed her face into his neck and he cupped the back of her head to keep her close.

"Did you know that Jonas made me promise to watch over you until you remarried?"

She shook her head, but didn't speak.

"He did. Two days before he died, he made me promise to see you happily wed before I left town. He knew I wanted to go west. You know what else I think he knew? I think he knew that I was in love with you years before I knew it myself."

"Really?" She drew back to look up at him.

"I believe that."

"He was always thinking of others. I loved that about him."

"I love him, too, you know."

"Maybe he hoped I would eventually see the fine man hidden behind the shy boy who could barely speak to me."

Levi shook his head. "We are a sad pair, you and I. I was afraid to speak for fear of looking the fool. You're afraid to love because it may bring you more loss. Neither one of us trusted God enough to lay our fears at His feet and ask what He wished of us. I found my voice because of you, Sarah."

"You found it because you wanted to help the children. You're right about one thing. I need to give over my burden and trust in His mercy. I'm just not sure I can."

"Yes, you can. Close your eyes and feel His love. I feel it and it gives me comfort."

"Levi, when did you know you loved me?"

He sighed. "I knew it the day you gave me a haircut. You could have plucked out my hairs one by one and I would have endured it without a peep. I've never wanted anything as much as I wanted your touch."

"But what if in a few months or a few years you discover Leah or Sally is the woman God wants for you?"

"You're right. I should test my feelings." He smiled at her and then lowered his face and kissed her.

Swept away in the glorious sensation of his lips on her, of his body pressed against hers, Sarah gave herself over to delight. She never wanted it to end. She wanted Levi to hold her forever and she wasn't afraid. This was so right. Her doubts slipped away as she gave her fear over to God.

Levi drew back a few seconds later. Her mind was still spinning. "Shall we test this some more?" he asked.

She nodded and lifted her face to his. The second kiss

was every bit as wonderful as the first. More wonderful, because she knew what was coming.

When he drew away again, he was as breathless as she was. "Tell me now that you don't love me."

He kissed her again before she could answer. When he drew away, she raised her arms to pull his head down to her and buried her fingers in his curls. Her crutches fell away, but she didn't need them. Levi was holding her up.

He placed a kiss on her forehead. "Say it, Sarah."

He placed another kiss on her eye. "Say it."

He nuzzled her cheek with his mouth a fraction of an inch from her wanting lips. "Say it, Sarah. I need to hear it."

"I love you, Levi Beachy."

"I knew you did."

A great weight lifted from her heart and she knew this was part of God's plan for her life. She smiled at Levi. He bent toward her and she raised her face for his kiss.

A long time later, she sighed and snuggled against him. He asked, "Are you cold?"

"Not a bit. I could stay here for hours."

"Your family will be missing you soon."

"I know, but can't we stay a little longer?" She never wanted this closeness to end. How blessed she was to have this second chance to love and be loved.

He looked over his shoulder. "I'm afraid we're about to be interrupted. My brothers are coming this way."

She took a step back and gave a small cry of pain.

He grasped her to keep her from falling and held her close. "Is it your knee?"

She nodded. "I reckon I've been up on it too long."

He wrapped his arm around her waist. "Lean on me. I will help you back to your house, unless I need to carry you."

She kept her face pressed against his shoulder. Breathlessly, she said, "I think you had better carry me."

He swung her up into his arms. "This is getting to be a habit."

She nuzzled his neck. "It's a habit I quite enjoy."

Levi stared into her eyes so full of love for him. "Tomorrow is Christmas Eve."

Sadness filled her eyes briefly, but it faded as she looked up at him. "I know."

"You haven't asked me what sort of gift I might like."

"Let me guess, a new rod and reel?"

"Not even close. All I want is your answer to a very important question, but I want it today, before Christmas. Will you marry me, Sarah Wyse?"

She bit her lip, then nodded. "I will."

He swung her around as joy pushed aside the last doubt from his heart. When she shrieked, he stopped and kissed her again. "Thank you. That is truly the best Christmas gift I have ever received."

"How soon are we moving to Colorado?" she asked with a grin.

He looked at her in surprise. "Just like that you're willing to go to Colorado? To leave all your friends and family? It might be years before we can come back for a visit."

"I know it will not be an easy thing, but I want you to follow your dream. You follow it. I will follow you."

"The decision is that simple for you?"

"I reckon it's as simple as can be. I want you to rise each morning and see God's glory in the mountains from our front porch."

He no longer needed to run away from the woman he couldn't have. "I've changed my mind about that."

"Really? Why?"

"Because God, in His goodness, has delivered to me

something more beautiful than the highest mountains. I won't even have to walk out on my porch to see it. My beautiful wife, my best Christmas gift, will be lying beside me in our bed each morning when I open my eyes. Wherever you are, Sarah Wyse, there is my heart, my dreams, my very life."

He bent and kissed her once more.

## Epilogue

When Sarah woke the morning of her wedding, she was tired but happy. Rushing to her window, she saw the sky outside was overcast with low gray clouds. The threat of snow hung in the air.

She crossed the room and opened her cedar chest. She took out the blue dress she had made with loving care years before. Her wedding dress. It would be the dress she would be buried in. She chose to wear it again for one simple reason. For Jonas.

He was the reason that she and Levi had fallen in love. If he hadn't asked Levi to stay and watch over her, Levi would have gone to Colorado and she might never have grown to love him. By wearing her first wedding dress, she was acknowledging her first husband's love and caring.

Her sprained knee had healed well enough in the two weeks since the accident that she could stand for small amounts of time and walk short distances. She was determined to stand unaided at her own wedding.

When she finally stepped down from her buggy at her aunt's house, she couldn't believe how nervous she was. Faith and Grace accompanied her. Sarah clenched her hands together and drew a deep breath.

"What's the matter?" Grace asked.

"My hands are like ice. I have butterflies the size of geese flopping around in my stomach."

Grace shook her head. "I can't believe you're nervous. You've done this before."

Faith gave her a hug. "I understand exactly how you feel."

Sarah knew that was true. Faith was also a widow who had found a new love in their small community.

"I think I'm more nervous than when I married Jonas. I don't know why I'm scared. I want nothing more than to spend the rest of my life with Levi."

Faith gave her a tiny push toward the front of her aunt's house. "That will not happen if you stand out here all day."

Sarah said, "Wait. It's starting to snow."

Grace looked up. "It is."

Flakes as large as duck down began floating to earth. They clung to Sarah's coat and settled around her feet. More and more followed until the air was thick with them.

Faith said, "We should go in. Everyone is waiting."

Sarah held out her hand and smiled at the white flakes sticking to her mittens. She looked out over the farm. The tall pine trees were catching the powdery fluff in their needles. She smiled at Grace. "Hear how quiet it has become? Isn't it beautiful?"

"Yes, it is," Faith agreed.

Jonas had loved the way snow turned the world into something clean and bright. Perhaps he had arranged this for her, a new start to her new life.

She said, "I used to hate the snow. There was snow on the ground when Jonas died, but from this day on, snowflakes will always remind me of my wedding day. I'm ready now."

Inside her aunt's home, the walls had been pushed back

to open up the downstairs rooms. Benches were arranged in two rows, men on one side and women on the other just as they were for regular preaching services.

Levi, looking remarkably handsome in his new black suit, white shirt and black bow tie, waited beside his brothers at the front of the room. The look in his eyes said everything she wanted to hear. Her nerves quieted and she walked toward her place at the front of the house beside Levi.

Sarah reached for Levi's hand. He gave her fingers a quick squeeze. Soon they would be joined as husband and wife.

As Sarah stood before Bishop Zook with Levi at her side, she knew the questions that would be asked of her.

Looking at them both, the bishop said, "Do you confess and believe God has ordained marriage to be a union between one man and one woman? And do you believe that you are approaching this marriage in accordance with His wishes and in the way you have been taught?"

She and Levi said, "Yes," in loud, clear voices.

Turning to Levi, the bishop asked, "Do you believe, brother, that God has provided this woman as a marriage partner for you?"

"Yes." Levi smiled at her and her heart beat faster.

The bishop then turned to her. "Do you believe, sister, that God has provided this man as a marriage partner for you?"

"Yes, I do."

"Levi, do you also promise Sarah that you will care for her in sickness or bodily weakness as befits a Christian husband and do you promise you will love, forgive and be patient with her until God separates you by death?"

"I do so promise," Levi answered solemnly.

"Sarah, do you promise the same, to care for Levi in

bodily weakness or sickness, as befits a Christian wife? Do you promise to love, forgive and be patient with him until God separates you by death?"

The question gave her pause. She knew it was coming, but she was still unprepared for the shaft of fear that hit her.

Would she someday be called upon to watch Levi die? Could she go through that agony again?

"Sarah?" the bishop prompted gently. He was waiting for her answer. The sympathy in his eyes said he understood her hesitation.

She focused on Levi. He was waiting, too.

Taking a deep breath, she nodded. She would be blessed to care for this man no matter how many or how few days were given to them. She raised her chin and said, "I promise."

The bishop smiled and nodded. He took her hand, placed it in Levi's hand and covered their fingers with his own. "The God of Abraham, of Isaac, and of Jacob be with you. May He bestow His blessings richly upon you through Jesus Christ, Amen."

She smiled brightly at Levi as he squeezed her hand. That was it. They were man and wife.

When the ceremony ended, the festivities began. Levi had but a moment to realize he was the luckiest man alive before he was quickly led away by his groomsmen. Looking over his shoulder, he saw Sarah being shepherded away by his sister and Faith Lapp.

The women of the congregation moved to the kitchen and started getting ready to serve dinner. The men arranged tables in a U-shape around the walls of the living room.

In the corner of the room facing the front door, the honored place, the *Eck,* meaning the corner table, was quickly set up for the wedding party.

When it was ready, Levi took his place with his groomsmen seated to his right. Sarah was ushered back in and
took her seat at his left-hand side. It symbolized the place
she would occupy in his buggy and in his life. Her cheeks
were rosy red and her eyes sparkled with happiness. They
clasped hands underneath the table. She was everything
he could have asked for and more.

There would be a long day of celebration and feast-
ing, but tonight would come, and she would be his alone.

Moses elbowed him in the side. "Put your tongue back
in your head *bruder,* you look like a panting dog. Greet
your guests."

Still unable to believe how blessed he was, Levi released Sarah's hand and began to speak to the people who
filed past.

The single men were arranged along the table to his
right and the single women were arranged along the tables
to Sarah's left. Later, for the evening meal, the young, unmarried people would be paired up according to the bride
and groom's choosing.

Levi leaned over. "You will have a chance to sharpen
your matchmaking skills this evening."

"My skills are sharp enough. I found you a wife,
didn't I?"

"*Ja,* and a right fine wife she is."

"I wonder who would do for Joann?"

"Look for a fellow with his own fly rod and a full tackle
box."

Sarah rolled her eyes and shook her head. "Men are
so limited in their thinking when it comes to matters of
the heart."

"Are you saying I don't have matchmaking skills?"

"Let us see. Who do you want to pair with Amos
Fisher?"

"Leah. I think she could make a silk purse out of a sow's ear."

"No. Leah needs someone quite special. I'll have to think on that one. Oh, I see Roman Weaver coming this way."

The pale young man stopped in front of them. He wore a sling. A thick cast covered his right arm. Sarah had heard he would never recover the full use of it. He said, "I wanted to thank you and your brothers for helping my family with my hospital bills."

"It was our pleasure, Roman," Sarah assured him.

"You would do the same for us," Levi added.

As Roman walked away, Sarah said, "I wonder if he and Joann know each other?"

"Ah, Sarah, one thing I know for sure. My life will never be boring with you by my side."

She smiled brightly and his heart turned over with happiness. "Say it again, my wife."

"Levi." She blushed and looked to see who might have noticed.

"Say it, Sarah, please."

She didn't even pretend to misunderstand. Leaning close, she whispered in his ear. "I love you, Levi Beachy, for now and for always."

It was exactly what his heart needed to hear.

\* \* \* \* \*

Dear Reader,

I hope you have enjoyed *A Hope Springs Christmas*. I was happy to help widow Sarah Wyse and Levi Beachy find the love they so richly deserved. I'm a big believer in love. Not just the love that makes a person go weak in the knees when they kiss. That kind of love is a wonderful way to start a relationship, but the love that grows over time and endures trials and challenges, that's the love I want my characters to find.

*A Hope Springs Christmas* is the seventh book I've written about the Amish in this fictional town. I feel as if I've come to know them, their funny quirks and their deep abiding faith. I hope you feel as if you know them, too.

Will there be more Hope Springs stories? I hope so, because Leah deserves to find her one true love, and I know that Joann could hook a winner if she used the right bait. Mary Shetler had such a troubled start to motherhood. She needs to find a young man who can see past her mistakes and be a father to her child. And Sally? That girl has secrets and doubts that she hides behind her endless questions. She'll need a strong man of faith to match her strong will. I'm not sure who it will be. I do know this, love springs eternal in Hope Springs, Ohio.

Blessings,

Patricia Davids

# Questions for Discussion

1. Sarah used her devotion to her job to keep from facing the sadness she felt each holiday season. Are the holidays difficult for you or someone you know? What can you do to help?

2. Grace was so worried about how her family would manage without her that she put her own happiness on hold. Do you sometimes feel smothered by the demands of your family? How can you make time for yourself?

3. Sarah discovered something she didn't know about Levi in chapter three. What was it? Why was it important?

4. Was Sarah right or wrong in her attempt to show the twins she disapproved of their behavior toward Henry? Should she have left it to Levi? What was it about his relationship with his brothers that began to change when Sarah refused to have them over to lunch?

5. Levi believes Gideon is mistaken when he suggests Levi is harboring deeper feelings toward Sarah. Have you seen two people you sense are falling in love? What gives them away?

6. Levi doesn't feel he fits in with the people around him at the church service even though he's known them all his life. Was it because he had to grow up too soon? What is one way we can foster a feeling

of togetherness in people so that they don't feel excluded in our churches?

7. The stunt the twins pulled with Dan and Susan Hershberger was funny, but it could have turned to be a tragedy. Have you ever done something you thought would be funny only to have it backfire? What happened?

8. Do you know a prankster like the twins? What would you like to say to them?

9. Sarah worked hard at matchmaking for Levi, but to no avail. Have you ever tried your hand at matchmaking? Have you set up a family member or friend with someone you thought they would like? How did it go? Would you try again?

10. I love fishing. I would choose fishing over almost any activity. What is your favorite pastime? Are you a quilter? A baker? What would you do if you were faced with engaging in an activity you didn't like, but had to do it for a friend?

11. Sarah was afraid to love again because she feared losing that person. Have you or someone you know suffered the "death" of love through divorce or loss of a spouse? How difficult is it to overcome the doubts that follow such an event? How does a person begin to believe in love again?

12. The gathering of women for a quilting bee or frolic is one of the iconic images we think of when we think of the Amish. Are the quilts made by many hands

less valuable than the quilts made by a single person? What determines the value of a quilt in your eyes?

13. What passage or phrase in this story resonated the most with you? Why?

14. Which characters would you like to revisit and why?

15. What did you like the most about this story?

# REQUEST YOUR FREE BOOKS!

## 2 FREE INSPIRATIONAL NOVELS
## PLUS 2
## FREE
## MYSTERY GIFTS

**YES!** Please send me 2 FREE Love Inspired® novels and my 2 FREE mystery gifts (gifts are worth about $10). After receiving them, if I don't wish to receive any more books, I can return the shipping statement marked "cancel." If I don't cancel, I will receive 6 brand-new novels every month and be billed just $4.49 per book in the U.S. or $4.99 per book in Canada. That's a saving of at least 22% off the cover price. It's quite a bargain! Shipping and handling is just 50¢ per book in the U.S. and 75¢ per book in Canada.* I understand that accepting the 2 free books and gifts places me under no obligation to buy anything. I can always return a shipment and cancel at any time. Even if I never buy another book, the two free books and gifts are mine to keep forever.

105/305 IDN FEGR

| | | |
|---|---|---|
| Name | (PLEASE PRINT) | |
| Address | | Apt. # |
| City | State/Prov. | Zip/Postal Code |

Signature (if under 18, a parent or guardian must sign)

Mail to the **Reader Service:**
**IN U.S.A.:** P.O. Box 1867, Buffalo, NY 14240-1867
**IN CANADA:** P.O. Box 609, Fort Erie, Ontario L2A 5X3

Not valid for current subscribers to Love Inspired books.

**Are you a subscriber to Love Inspired books
and want to receive the larger-print edition?
Call 1-800-873-8635 or visit www.ReaderService.com.**

* Terms and prices subject to change without notice. Prices do not include applicable taxes. Sales tax applicable in N.Y. Canadian residents will be charged applicable taxes. Offer not valid in Quebec. This offer is limited to one order per household. All orders subject to credit approval. Credit or debit balances in a customer's account(s) may be offset by any other outstanding balance owed by or to the customer. Please allow 4 to 6 weeks for delivery. Offer available while quantities last.

**Your Privacy**—The Reader Service is committed to protecting your privacy. Our Privacy Policy is available online at www.ReaderService.com or upon request from the Reader Service.

We make a portion of our mailing list available to reputable third parties that offer products we believe may interest you. If you prefer that we not exchange your name with third parties, or if you wish to clarify or modify your communication preferences, please visit us at www.ReaderService.com/consumerschoice or write to us at Reader Service Preference Service, P.O. Box 9062, Buffalo, NY 14269. Include your complete name and address.

LIREG11B

## SPECIAL EXCERPT FROM
## LOVE INSPIRED® SUSPENSE

*Brave police officers tackle crime with the help of their canine partners in* TEXAS K-9 UNIT, *an exciting new series from Love Inspired® Suspense.*

*Read on for a preview of the first book,*
*TRACKING JUSTICE by Shirlee McCoy.*

Police detective Austin Black glanced at his dashboard clock as he raced up Oak Drive. Two in the morning. Not a good time to get a call about a missing child.

Then again, there was never a good time for that; never a good time to look in the worried eyes of a parent or to follow a scent trail and know that it might lead to a joyful reunion or a sorrowful goodbye.

*If* it led anywhere.

Sometimes trails went cold, scents were lost and the missing were never found. Austin wanted to bring them all home safe. Hopefully, this time, he would.

He pulled into the driveway of a small house.

Justice whined. A three-year-old bloodhound, he was trained in search and rescue and knew when it was time to work.

Austin jumped out of the vehicle when a woman darted out the front door. "You called about a missing child?"

"Yes. My son. I heard Brady call for me, and when I walked into his room, he was gone." She ran back up the porch stairs.

Austin jogged in after her. She waved from a doorway. "This is my son's room."

Austin followed her into the room. "How old is your son, Ms….?"

"Billows. Eva. He's seven."

"Did you argue?"

"We didn't argue about anything, Officer…"

"Detective Austin Black. I'm with Sagebrush Police Department's Special Operation K-9 Unit."

"You have a search dog with you?" Her face brightened. "I can give you something of his. A shirt or—"

"Hold on. I need to get a little more information first."

"How about you start out there?" She gestured to the window.

"Was it open when you came in the room?"

"Yes. It looks like someone carried Brady out the window. But I don't know how anyone could have gotten into his room when all the doors and windows were locked."

"You're sure?"

"Of course." She frowned. "I always double-check. I have ever since…"

"What?"

"Nothing that matters. I just need to find my son."

Hiding something?

"Everything matters when a child is missing, Eva."

*To see Justice the bloodhound in action, pick up*
*TRACKING JUSTICE by Shirlee McCoy.*
*Available January 2013 from Love Inspired® Suspense.*

# Linda Goodnight

brings you a tale of a cowboy you can trust.

Rancher Austin Blackwell sees Annalisa Keller as a wounded
person with too many secrets. This town is the perfect
place for her to start over—just as it was for him. Trying to
keep his own past hidden, Austin finds himself falling for
Annalisa, whose warmth and love of life works its way
into his heart…and promises never to leave.

# Rancher's Refuge

Where every prayer is answered….

*Available December 2012, wherever books are sold.*

www.LoveInspiredBooks.com

LI87787